THE
AWKWARD SQUADS
and selected short stories

THE
AWKWARD SQUADS
and selected short stories

Shan Bullock

TURNPIKE BOOKS

This selection © Turnpike Books 2013

'The Awkward Squads' and 'A State Official' first published in *The Awkward Squads and other stories*, Cassell and Company (1893); 'They That Mourn', 'The Emigrant', 'The Splendid Shilling' and 'Shan's Diversion' first published in *Ring O' Rushes*, Ward, Lock & Co (1896); 'The Herd' first published in *Irish Pastorals*, Grant Richards (1901).

turnpikebooks@gmail.com

ISBN 9780957233645

This book is sold subject to the condition that it shall not, by way of trade or otherwise, be lent, re-sold, hired out, or otherwise circulated without the publisher's prior consent in any form of binding or cover other than that in which it is published and without a similar condition including this condition being imposed on the subsequent purchaser.

This publication may not be reproduced, stored in a retrieval system, or transmitted, in any form or by any means, electronic, mechanical, photocopying, recording or otherwise, without the prior permission of the publisher.

Typeset by RefineCatch Ltd, Bungay, Suffolk

Printed and bound by MPG Printgroup Limited, UK

CONTENTS

The Awkward Squads	1
A State Official	73
They That Mourn	84
The Emigrant	92
Shan's Diversion	99
The Splendid Shilling	108
The Herd	126
Biography	151

THE AWKWARD SQUADS

I

Not very long ago, about eight o'clock one night in early spring, certain men in the townland of Bilboa, county Cavan, left their homes and set their faces towards the house of one James O'Gara. Though the night was lowering, and the moon yet young beneath the clouds, all kept well away from the lanes and roads which run through that wild and thinly-populated country. Anyone, by chance, seeing them steal through the whins and rushes, and along the ditches and hedges, would have scented poteen or poaching in the wind.

As each sighted his destination he pulled his hat over his eyes, buttoned his coat, pocketed his pipe, and, skirting the dwelling-house, made for the door of the barn in the back-yard. There he knocked thrice, spoke once, and quickly vanished.

At twenty minutes past eight twenty-five men had assembled in O'Gara's barn, filling it to the door. At one end of the rough, clay-floored building a plank laid on two trestles bore a couple of candles stuck in empty whisky bottles, and fronted the burly figure of Michael Dooley, Esq., P.L.G. On the opposite wall hung a tin sconce in which a tallow dip flared and guttered. Between the lights was the audience, seated on stools, chairs, forms, and all things handy. To the right of the table sat a young man with an inkpot in his hand and on his knee a note-book, in which, as each man passed the doorkeeper, he had entered the new comer's name. He had a keen face, his eyes were restless, and his appearance went far to explain why, among his neighbours, he was known as *Mister* Farrell.

Suddenly, he looked at his watch, drew a heavy line underneath the list of names, and rose.

"Boys," he said, "least said soonest mended. I propose Mr. Dooley to the chair. Who seconds that?"

"I do," said a voice from the back.

"All o' ye for that howld up your hands," said Mr. Farrell. "*One, two, three—eighteen*. All against put up your hands. *None*. Mr. Dooley——"

"I propose yirself," said a voice.

"Whisht, whisht," said Mr. Farrell, "no foolin'! Mr. Dooley, this meetin', *nem. con.*, has moved ye to the chair."

Mr. Dooley rose, inclined his body forward, and sat down again. The honour was but his due; he was the guest of the evening; the meeting well knew (so he thought) that he was the only man in the barn who could fill the chair with dignity and force. He pulled his chair up to the table, and shifted the candles nearer him.

"Somewon," he said from his seat, "stand outside an' watch."

The door opened, and Barney Cafferty went out.

"Somewon," said the Chairman, "bar the door an' admit nowon."

Micky Dolan shot the bolt and set his broad back against the door.

"Fire away!" Micky said. "All's secure."

"Mr. Farrell," the Chairman said, "call the roll."

Mr. Farrell put his inkpot and pen beside the candle-bottle and, rising, asked the lads to answer up and show their hands. As each name was called, its owner, answering "Here," put up his right hand and held it there till the next name was read.

"Have I called ye all?" asked Mr. Farrell when he had read through his list. There was no answer.

"How many did ye admit, Micky Dolan?" he asked.

"Twenty-foive includin' meself an' Barney Cafferty outside," said Micky.

Mr. Farrell mounted his chair and counted the audience, pointing at each with the end of his pen. "*One, two, three . . . twenty-four*. Right."

He sat down, drew a line through the row of names, signed the page, and passed the book to the Chairman. Mr. Dooley squared himself at the table, took the pen in his clumsy fingers, and, after a preliminary flourish in the air, wrote his name in a sprawling shop-hand. That feat over, he cleared his throat and rose. He was a big, pompous man, full of the self-sufficiency and the ideas proper to a Guardian of the Poor, a promising politician, a local satellite, and a moneyed man.

As he faced the rows of keen, watching faces, he threw back his shoulders and calmly eyed his audience; then stooped slightly, pressed his open palms on the board before him, and began.

"Gentlemin," he said, and forthwith straightened himself and crossed his hands before him. "Gentlemin, this is not the first, nor is it the second, nor, I will dare to add, is it the last occasion

I have addressed, or will address you." His voice was florid; and all his art could not smother the broad, unctuous brogue.

"Gentlemin," he went on, throwing open his coat, "we have met here the night in a tremend*u*ous an' ard*u*ous cause." He rolled his lips round the sounding words. "I stand here before ye as yir chairman, yir *u*nanimously *e*lected chairman, proud av the honour av addressin' you; proud-m-av—gloryin' in the principles we share together; rejoicin' in the bond av union that binds uz together: *yet*," his voice sought its gravest depths, "I confess, weighed down by the solemnity, the gravity, the *por*tentousness of me thoughts." He paused for a brief space, then pressed his right hand to his side and spouted with his left. "For what are we met together? What voice calls uz? What arrm beckons uz? What *cause* claims uz? Gentlemin, the voice av DUTY calls: the arrm av FREEDOM beckons: and-a the cause av IRELAND claims uz." He stooped and mouthed his words at the faces before him. There was a sound of shifting feet and deep breathing throughout the barn. The expected applause did not come. A smoker in the middle of the room struck a match on his pipe-bowl and lit up the comically puzzled faces around him.

"Gentlemin," Mr. Dooley went on, "we are this day an enloightened nation. Oideas are in th' air, gentlemin; from the Giants' Causeway to the Cove av Cork th' air is full av oideas that fall on enloightened minds. We are a yunited nation; we are an awakened nation; we have spurned the fut av the oppressor, an' risen lek the young aigle o' the mornin'."

Someone groaned in his distress; the audience moved restlessly; a second match lit up faces that were almost grinning. Mr. Farrell writhed where he sat and nervously fingered his pen.

"But, gentlemin," Mr. Dooley went on, "our upward flight is not unimpeded; our career is not unenvied; our progress is not unobstructed. Gentlemin, inimies—*inimies*, I repeat—are around uz. There are those who wid shackle our arrms wi' the chains av slaves; wid cut our pinions; wid take their fut off our necks only to put a rope roun' them; will—I say *will*—prevent, as much as in them lies, the achievement of our liberties an' our roights as a nation. Gentlemin, ye all know the history of our past. In the year seventeen hundred an'———"

Here someone put his head on his hands and cried: "Och, och!" and at once the meeting broke out into murmurings. The unsteady flare of the candles fell on forms and faces and hands in a state of ferment. Mr. Farrell jumped up with a snap.

"Here, enough of this———" he began.

Mr. Dooley waved him back. "Easy, easy," he said. "Leave it to me. What's the matter, gentlemin? What's the offence? Am I addressin' friends?"

"Ye are, ye are," some cried. "Talk sinse," cried others. "We want talk, not bleather," said Micky Dolan, standing with his back to the door. "Hear, hear," went up the voices. "That's it!" "Talk straight!" "Damn yir blarney!"

The Chairman spread out his hands. "Gentlemin, gentlemin," he said, "let me beg av you———"

"Gentlemin be hanged!" said Micky Dolan. "We're only plain stirabout lek yirself. This is no Board-room. Spake up, Mr. Farrell."

"Ay, ay!" cried the voices. "Spake up, Mister Farrell."

Farrell got upon his chair. "Lads," he said, "be conny; be aisy; don't be bleathers yourselves. Whisht a bit an' I'll———"

Mr. Dooley raised his voice in interruption.

"Arrah whisht wid ye, ye oul' grampus ye," said Micky Dolan; "you an' yir divil's bleather! Sit down, sor!"

"Down wid ye!" went up the chorus; and, amid jeers and skirls, Michael Dooley, Esq., sat down.

"Boys," Mr. Farrell went on, "aisy, aisy. Mr. Dooley means well, but we're not well used to his style o' spache. We'd lek well to hear his powerful langwidge some other night when we've more time. We're in a hurry the night, Mr. Dooley, an', if you'll excuse me, sir, I'll put the case in a word or two."

"Certainly, certainly, Mr. Farrell," Mr. Dooley said. "Please don't think I'm at all perturbed."

"Well, lads," said Mr. Farrell, "there's no need to say much. Ye all know most as much as meself. I needn't go back on history to fin' me words. Puttin' things straight, here's the case: Wid the help o' God, 'fore very long we'll ha' Irelan' a Nation an' a Parlemint on College Green." The meeting straightened up and gave the speaker an encouraging skirl. "That's what *we* say," Mr. Farrell went on in his vigorous, fluent way, "an' *th' others* say: 'Wi' the help o' God, we'll never knuckle under or obey any Parlemint o' yours on College Green.' 'Won't ye, begorra?' sez we. 'Wait an' see!' 'Be damned to us,' sez they; 'but we'll fight ye first; we'll rise the North agin ye; we'll cut yir throats: we'll line the ditches an' defy ye!' That's what *they* say."

The meeting sent up a derisive howl.

"Well, lads, that's straight," Mr. Farrell continued. "We know the worst an' we know the best. Will they fight? Mebbe so, an' mebbe not; most likely not. Divil cares! Here's the point—*if they fight, we must be ready for them.* I hear they're drillin', an' gettin' rifles, an' catridges, an' divil knows what; an' the newspapers are backin' them up. What are we to do? *Get ready ourselves, me sons! Drill! Get guns! Prepare!* Isn't that it?"

"Good, me son," went up the voices. "That's the kin' o' talk!" "Bravo, bravo!"

"An' that's what we're goin' to do, me sons, isn't it?" said Mr. Farrell.

"Ay, ay!"

"An' that's what we've come here the night for, me sons?"

"Ay, ay!"

"Then to blazes wid talk, an' let's to business!" Mr. Farrell stepped from his seat.

"Terry Fitch," he said, "step forrad."

A short, powerfully-built man, with a round, cropped head and square face, made his way from the back of the barn and stood straight and square as a tower before Mr. Farrell.

"Ye mind most o' your militia drill, Terry, I'll warrant?" said Mr. Farrell.

"Most av ut," said Terry.

"Could ye tache what ye know?"

"I cud."

"D'ye think ye could lick the lads into shape now?"

"If they're willin', an' have sinse."

"How many could ye manage at once?"

Terry looked round.

"As many, mebbe, as there's here."

"Twenty or thirty or that?"

"Ay."

"Will ye try?"

"I will."

"Lads," Mr. Farrell said to the meeting, "I propose Terry Fitch as our drill sergeant. Does that suit ye?"

"Yis," went up the voices.

"No objections? That's right. Terry, you're appointed—the right man in the right place. Mr. Dooley, sir, I hope you're pl'ased?"

"Oh, yes, yes," said the deposed Chairman. "Yes, yes. Pray don't mind me."

"We'll want a kin' o' committee now, lads," said Farrell, "jist to keep their eye on things. Fire out the names now."

"Yirself for one," said a voice. Chosen unanimously.

"James O'Gara as another," said a voice. Also chosen.

"Micky Reilly as a third, an' a dacent man," said Micky Dolan. Also chosen.

"Micky Dolan himself," said Micky Reilly. Chosen.

"Shan Grogan, a thrue man," said a voice. "Ay, ay!" was the chorus. Chosen.

Mr. Farrell held up his hand.

"Lads, you've now got five," he said, "an' six 'll do. I put to ye as the last one, an' not the least, the name of our rispected chair, Mr. Dooley."

This was a politic proposal, and one that, after a little hesitation and a few outspoken criticisms, was given the sanction of the meeting.

"The Committee 'll come forrad," said Mr. Farrell. And at once the honoured members took their places in front of the meeting.

"First," said Mr. Farrell addressing his colleagues, "mebbe we'd better give our instructions to Terry Fitch."

"What's that?" said Terry.

"Give ye your instructions," said Mr. Farrell.

"What d'ye mane?" asked Terry.

"Tell ye what you're to do."

Terry laughed.

"Faith an' yi'd better try, shure," he said. "Mebbe yi'll drill the Squad as well?"

"Whist, Terry," said Shan Grogan, "an' don't be fractious, man!"

"Fractious is it ye say, Shan Grogan?" said Terry. "An' who's fractious? Who here's able to instruct me, I'd lek to know?"

"No one, Terry," said Mr. Farrell, "an' no one wants to. Arrah, what ails ye? What is it ye want?"

"To do me own work me own way."

"But the Committee——"

"Committee be blowed!" said Terry. "What does the Committee know av drill?"

"Sorra hate, Terry," said Mr. Farrell; "but it knows other things."

"Well, let it attind to th' other things an' lave me alone," said Terry.

Mr. Farrell scratched his head. "Look here, Terry," he said, "don't spoil fun. Speak out! What is it ye want?"

"Put yir Squad in a roomy, convenient, safe place an' let me at it," said Terry. "That's all. I'll do me juty, niver fear. But I want no instructin' be Committ*ee*s."

"An' why the blazes didn't ye say that at wanst, ye gawm, ye?" said Micky Dolan. "Wastin' our precious time lek this! It's chucked ye shud be!"

"What's that avick?" said Terry.

"I said *chucked*, pitched out o' the place; is that straight?"

Terry took off his coat and began rolling up his shirt sleeves.

"All right," he began, "chuck me!"

"Lads, lads," Mr. Farrell cried, "keep quiet an' don't be ijuts! Terry, put on your coat! Micky, hold your gab! Both of ye sit down! Boys," he cried to the meeting, "sit down! What Terry says is rasonable. Let's drop that. Where's the best place to meet?"

One proposed here, one there; all were unsuitable. Then Mr. Dooley rose, and, with a fine condescension in his manner and a grieved tremor in his voice, said that to his poor mind the most suitable place for their purpose, the safest and most roomy, was the old castle across Thrasna river on the top of Rhamus hill.

"That's in Fermanagh," said one. "The inimies' country!" said another. "All the better," said a third. "It's beyant the river," said a fourth. "It's the place, the only place," said Terry Fitch; "it's safe, an' convenient, an' roomy." Terry's word settled the matter, and Mr. Dooley leaned back in his chair well pleased.

Next the Committee fixed the date of the first drill—the following Saturday night at half-past eight to catch the moon.

Then they settled upon a small subscription to cover current expenses; arranged the drill nights; gave instructions that word should be passed round the country-side with a view to the formation of other Squads; appointed Mr. Dooley their President and Mr. Farrell their Secretary; and drew up a set of rules to govern their movements. These things satisfactorily arranged, Mr. Farrell asked the meeting what weapons were at the disposal of the Committee.

"I've an ould blunderbuss in the corner yonder," said a voice from the back, "that'll kill dead if she carries straight; but she's oncertain."

"Troth an' I've a yoke av a fowlin' piece, too," said another, "that'll kill behind her if she doesn't in front. Faith an' I'd liefer be in front meself, bar accidents, for stren'th isn't her strong point."

"An' there's a horse-pistol an' a bay'net at home yonder on the loft," said a third, "if the childer hasn't swopped them."

"Hish!" said Mr. Farrell to the laughing meeting. "Hish! No foolishness. It's time enough to think o' weapons yit mebbe. The thing is to learn to use them. Isn't that it, Terry?"

"About it," Terry said. He spoke out to the meeting. "I want yis all to onderstand that no arrms av any class or description is to come at first to my drills. I've more regard for me personal safety; an' to carry arrms jist now is agin the law. But I'd lek yis to bring some article wid ye that 'd tache ye to use yir han's in a sojer-lek fashion—spade handles or scythe-sneds, or things o' that sort. But the first man I see wid fire-arrms, till I give instructions, 'll right about face wid me toe on his breeches. Come punctual, an' obey orders, an' polish up thim brains o' yours!"

Everything was now arranged; so with a vote of thanks to Mr. Dooley, and a vow of secrecy as each man passed out, the meeting dispersed.

II

The old castle on Rhamus hill, just across Thrasna river from Bilboa, is an admirable place for secret meetings of any kind. Poteen has been run there, and cocks fought, and heroic battles waged over the bright eyes of country-side beauties. The nearest house is an Irish mile away. Looking towards Bilboa one sees that the castle commands the county road on the right, Thrasna river in front, and a great swampy bog on the left. At the back is a fir plantation. The hill itself is steep and barren, with only whins and rushes on its sides, and great whitethorn hedges that run to the top and end at the ditch and hedge that enclose the castle walls. Within the ruined, ivy-covered battlements is a big, level grass-plot, that goes by the name of the Castle Green. The massive walls are pierced here and there by sloping loop-holes. On the plantation side part of the wall is levelled, and a large hole gapes towards Bilboa. Facing the river and the road are two round, loop-holed turrets, with narrow doorways facing inwards. Inside and out the ivy and brier and elder-tree flourish, whilst here and there on the walls a sapling springs amid the wild flowers. A lonelier spot could hardly be found, nor one easier to be attained without fear of detection. Certainly it was in the "enemies' country"—but what of that? Did not the fact inspire the Bilboa Squad with a pleasant sense of bravery and heroic recklessness?

Saturday night was fine and mild. The moon, dimly revealed in the cloudy sky, lent just sufficient light for the Squad's purpose. By cots and boats, and over Thrasna bridge, the men crossed the river, and stole in ones and twos by the hedge, up the hill, and through the hole in the castle walls. There they greeted each other, lit their pipes, and turned to the loop-holes to watch.

At fifteen minutes past eight the Twenty-five were on parade; and to the minute of half-past Terry Fitch crept through the hole and paced to the centre of the green. He was clad in an old grey overcoat, a Glengarry cap, corduroy trousers, and a pair of military highlows. In his hand he carried a short switch, and a corner of a red pocket-handkerchief peeped from the left sleeve of his great coat.

He put his switch under his arm, and drawing his heels together with a click, said, in a deep growl, "Squ-a-d, fall in!"

At the word, the Twenty-five pocketed their pipes, and, jostling each other in their clumsiness, gathered in a mob before Terry. His face darkened.

"Squ-a-d," he growled, "fall in two deep accordin' to size."

The men looked right and left, shifted their legs, and remained as they were.

"Squad," said Terry, "as ye were."

The Squad in its perplexity stood fast.

"Oh! blow ye," said Terry in disgust, "go back where ye wur afore I cem!"

The men broke up and went back.

"Phil Brady," growled Terry.

"Yis," said Phil.

"Come here, ye fool!"

Phil slouched forward.

"Stan' there," said Terry, "an' don't move till I tell ye. Howld up yir head, man. Keep yir knees straight, man. What's that yi've got in yir han'? A spade han'le is it? Thin drop it."

"Micky Dolan," growled Terry.

"Here," said Micky.

"Shiver ye! come when I tell ye."

Micky dropped his stick, came forward, and was placed by Phil Brady's side.

"What's that ye dropped?" asked Terry.

"Me weapon," said Micky.

"An' what for, ye wastrel, ye?"

"Bekase ye med Phil Brady do it," said Micky.

Terry groaned.

"Here," he said to the Squad, "all o'ye come forrad an' pile yir arrms. This way, this way," he shouted, "dang yir skins, this way! Put them down *here*! Now back wid ye."

Then, one by one, Terry called out his men and shoved them into their places. The result was two rows of very curious and very raw recruits. Terry eyed them doubtfully. Some were manly, stalwart youths; a few were old, stiffened men; the majority were middle-aged farmers—awkward, careworn, heavy-footed. One or two wore sleeved moleskin waistcoats, others long frieze overcoats, others ragged jackets; Mr. Farrell and Mr. Dooley were clad in rough tweed; the majority wore corduroy trousers fastened at the knee with hay ropes, or caught at the bottom in old leggings; and the prevailing head-dress was the familiar battered felt hat.

Suddenly Terry went to the walls and looked down the hill towards the river. "Be jabers," he said to himself, "I'm forgettin' meself! What's up wid me at all? Well, better late nor niver." He turned to the Squad and told off three men to mount guard outside the ditch that encircled the castle. One man faced the river, one the road, the third kept guard by the fir plantation. Their orders were "Keep yir eyes open, an' if ye see anything don't make a noise over it." The guard mounted, Terry went back to the Squad. Already some of the men were smoking, and had broken their ranks. Terry swooped on them.

"Ye divil's crew, ye," he cried, "put out thim pipes! Is it smokin' on parade y' are, ye crippled whelps, ye? Stan' to yir places, blast ye; howld up yir heads; straighten up, ye fools, ye!"—and so on. The Squad bore the fire bravely, and like heroes held their peace.

"Now min," said Terry, when he had recovered his temper, "I want jist to spake a few words to ye afore I commence on ye. The first juty av a sojer is to obey his commandin' officer. His next juty is to sharpen the wits that God gev him; if he doesn't they'll *be* sharpened, I tell ye."

As Terry spoke he paraded up and down before the Squad, his hands behind him and his eyes on the ranks.

"After that," he continued, "the sojer must try to *luk* like wan—turn his toes out, straighten his back, an' be clane an' dacent. What most av ye are goin' to turn out"—Terry stopped and eyed the ranks—"the Lord only knows. I misdoubt yi're as onlikely a lot as iver I clapped eyes on. Howsomedever I'm goin' to try me han' on ye, an' sich as I've gone through meself I'll put you through. James Reilly, for the love o' marcy try to luk like a man. Luk at me an' see how yi 're stan'in' ." Terry dropped a knee forward, loosened his back, hung his head, and let his arms fall before him. "Isn't that a charmin' view, James? Isn't that how yi'd lek to look in yir Sunday shuit afore the girls, James? *Silence in the ranks!* Who dar' laugh? The first man I see wid the shadda av a grin on him 'll do pack drill for an hour. I'm keepin' ye stan'in' lek y' are jist to make yis feel yirselves. If yir backs ache, all the better." He ran his eye down the front rank. "Och, och!" he said, "the sight av it! In an' out lek a gander's teeth! *Front rank, right dress!* Eyes right, ye blunderin' ijuts, ye! *Will* yis look at me? Howld up them *heads!* Stan' back there, Pat's Micky. Come up, will ye, Phil Brady. *E-y-e-s front!* Och, luk in front av ye for the love av marcy, an' don't be bigger gawms than y' are."

Again he took up his parade before the Squad.

"I'm not goin' to do much to yis the night," he said. "If yis l'arn to stan' quiet an' not flop so much 'll do. When the bugle soun's for drill the first juty av the sojer is to run lek blazes to parade. Wanst there he falls into his place in the ranks as natural as if he was led be a string. At the word '*Ah-tintion*,' he starches himself an' stans lek a post—lek this. At the word '*Stan'-at-ease*,' he lets himself go a bit an' stan's lek this. At the word '*Stan' easy*,' he throws himself loose entoirely.—*Squ-a-d*—Ah-*tintion!* Now then, han's straight be the side; heads up; heels togither; chests out, bellies in—Phil Brady, I've seen ijuts in me day, but the leks o' you I've yit to meet. You an' James Reilly shud be spanchelled togither lek a pair o' goats an' turned out to grass. Man alive, yir gran'mother was a better man nor you! Have ye any backbone at all in ye avick, or are ye stuffed wid bran?" Terry playfully poked the unfortunate Phil in the ribs. Phil lifted his hand.

"Terry Fitch," he said, "none o' yir foolery! Quit proddin' me, or I'll brek yir mouth. We've had too much o' yir clack the night."

Something like a murmur of approval ran up and down the ranks. Terry stepped back.

"Oho!" he said, "Oho! Insubordination in the ranks! Impidence to the commandin' officer! Be jabers an' I'll tache ye a lesson. Stan' forrad, Private Brady!"

"Divil the length o' me big toe, then!" said Phil.

"Private Brady," said Terry, "I give ye fair warnin'—stan' forrad, or take the consequinces."

"Divil a step," said Phil: "do yir worst."

Terry put down his cane, settled his cap firmly on his head, and walked up to Phil. The two clenched, and before Phil had time to breathe he was sprawling on his back in the middle of the green.

"That's better nor a dale o' talk," said Terry, as he picked up his switch. "*Squ-a-d, Ah*——"

But before the order was finished, and whilst Private Brady was yet resting on the grass, the river-guard put his head over the wall and said, "Whisht, boys, whisht! but there's three men joukin' up the hill be the hedge."

"*Squad*," said Terry, "*stan' fast*."

The Twenty-five checked themselves in their first impulse to run, and Terry went to take observations. Hardly had he turned his back when the road-guard put his head over the wall and said that two men were jouking up the hedge his side o' the hill. Instantly the Squad broke, and scrambling up the ivy, cautiously peered across the wall.

The alarm was only too true: five forms were rapidly approaching.

The Squad clambered down and, panic-stricken, ran here and there across the green.

"Squad," growled Terry, "retire on the plantation."

The Twenty-five gathered together and fled—only to meet the rear-guard bringing word that a man even then was skirting the far edge of the plantation. Surrounded on all sides, the Squad saw ruin impending. Terry alone kept cool.

"Lads," he said, "pick up yir weapons an' hide in the ivy on the top o' the walls."

Half a minute afterwards Rhamus Castle, to all appearance, was deserted.

Then from their places in the ivy the Twenty-five saw five of the "enemy" steal through the broken wall and, even as they themselves had done, take their stations by the loopholes and watch. Presently these were joined by others, till at last eighteen had assembled. And these in contented ignorance smoked and talked, whilst the Twenty-five on the walls wondered, and lay tight, and trembled.

A tall, white-haired man, with a flowing beard, came up the hill carrying a carpet-bag, entered the ruins, said "Fine night, men," and went straight to the river-turret. There he opened the bag and took out an old yeomanry shako, a red tunic, and a pair of white cotton gloves. Then he took off his coat and trousers (revealing a flannel shirt and a pair of loose white ducks) and put both garments into the bag. Lastly he donned the tunic and shako, fastened a purple sash across his right shoulder, pulled on his gloves, and thus attired stepped out on the moonlit green.

This was Samuel Mires, late sergeant in the Lowth Castle Infantry, a disbanded yeomanry corps whose commander and owner had been Lord Lowth, and whose modest motto, worn on their shakoes, had been "Croppies Lie Down."

Pausing about the middle of the green, Sergeant Mires cleared his throat, and drawing himself erect, said "Men, fall in." At once the Eighteen pocketed their pipes, the fumes of which for ten minutes or so had set the Bilboa men longing among the ivy, and drew up in two lines before the Sergeant. Their movements and quickness in finding their places showed that they had drilled before. Terry Fitch's opinion of the Squad—if, indeed, his sense of the absurdity of its instructor allowed him to watch it at all—probably was that he wished his own as good. The Eighteen certainly moved as eighteen men; they were clumsy and slow; there were points for the satirist about each—fatness, leanness, ugliness, shapelessness; the mark of the soldier was on none; yet all had passed from that stage of rawness which marks the untrained man. They were dressed somewhat better than were the Bilboa men, and their faces were such that had the two squads been mixed an outsider could have separated them at once. He would have put the clean-shaven Irish faces, with their keen features and restless eyes on one side; on the other he would have put the beards and whiskers, the men with memories of England and Scotland in their looks.

Sergeant Mires drew a book from his tunic and called the roll, ticking off the names of those who answered "Here." He read out about fifty names. Then he called the Squad to attention.

"I'm sorry to see so few here the night," he said in a clear, sharp voice. "I was expectin' more, seein' how fine it is. I hope the fallin' off won't continue, an' that all o' you 'll tell yir neighbours to come reg'lar an' often. Dis any o' ye know why they haven't come?"

"Work's throng this time o' the year," said Robert Young; "men ha' to work late an' rise early."

"We're one like another," answered Sergeant Mires; "but we must deny ourselves a little to save our principles."

"Saterday's a bad night," said John Gibson; "there's always odd jobs to be done for Sundays."

"Ay, an' it's market day," said James Harper; "people must sell to buy bits for their bellies."

"An' drink!" said big Ned Noble. "Marketin's powerful thirsty work."

The Eighteen, with their Sergeant, laughed, and the eyes of the Twenty-five glittered in the ivy at the thought of whisky.

"Well," said Sergeant Mires, "whatever may be the cause, I hope next time the muster 'll be better. It's discouragin' to you, an' it's discouragin' to me, to come here at some risk to ourselves an' some loss o' precious time, too, seein' the s'ason o' the year—to come here, I say, an' not have a good muster. Ye know it's no good doin' things be halves. What's the good o' me walkin' studdy in the ranks an' knowin' how to han'le me weapon, if me neighbour beside me's actin' lek an omadhaun—Is there now?"

"Well, sorra bit," said the Eighteen. "Bedad no." "Shure, yi're sp'akin' Gospel."

"An' if people stay away because they think nothin' 'll iver happen," went on the Sergeant, "I'd lek yis to spake yir minds to them an' tell them that the man is blessed who has his house in order. We're standin' on the edge av a vulcano. May the Lord grant it niver bursts! But if it does, we musn't be caught asleep. I hear strange talk flyin' about. People say *th' others* are drillin' too."

The Twenty-five cocking in the ivy bent all their ears.

"It's true," said James Harper. "I hear the talk everywhere."

"Talk's nothin'," said Ned Noble. "An' if so be, what odds? Eh, what odds? Let them drill away; but let them keep out of *our* way anyhow, drill or no drill. So say I."

"Easy, easy, Ned," said Sergeant Mires. "Keep down yir voice: it travels far. What I want to say is this: Bring yir neighbours here, that if iver the day *should* come that we be called on to fight an' defend ourselves an' our homes from onjust oppression, we may be found ready to do our juty an' scatter our foes lek chaff before the whirlwind."

"Hear, hear, hear," said Ned Noble; "that's the way to put it! Trust in God an' keep your powder dry, me boys!——

"*For we're the boys*," he chanted in a deep voice, "*that fear no noise, an' niver will surren-dur!*"

All this time the Bilboa men were wearying on the wall. They dared not move a leg for fear of loosening a stone or rustling the ivy. Mr. Dooley, in particular—resting as he was in a half-lying posture, leaning on one hand and grasping ivy stems with the other—was terribly uncomfortable. His limbs were cramped, his back ached, his great body felt full of pains. He longed for the drill to begin that he might have an opportunity to shift his position. Would they never cease talking!

Then Ned Noble's voice arose, and Mr. Dooley felt that his chance had come. Slowly he rolled his body over, slipped on a sloping stone, broke his hold on the ivy, and went with a crash to the ground outside. As he fell he clutched at the ivy and roared.

There was a sudden scurry inside the walls, a sound of feet clumping on the grass as the Bilboa men slipped from the ivy, and—the Twenty-five to the river, the Eighteen to the road— both Squads took to their heels and fled.

III

The stampede of the Twenty-five ended at the river. Shan Grogan was the first man to reach it; Terry Fitch was the last.

Half-way down the hill, Terry, in jumping a ditch, hit a stone with his toe and fell. The fall, whilst leaving him far behind in the retreat, also helped him to recover his wits, and thenceforward he walked soberly, and gained courage at every step. He even brought himself in the end to look scornfully at the straggling, flying line that marked the flight of the Twenty-five. He reached the river-bank with a calm, easy stride; his cap jauntily cocked, his cane tapping his leg. Most of the Squad, in a hopelessly demoralised state, were running here and there to find room in the boats. Mr. Dooley sat panting and groaning on the grass. Mr. Farrell alone preserved some appearance of steadiness. Terry drew out his pipe, lit up, and marched for the nearest boat. Seven men were already in it, and one on the bank was vainly trying to push it off.

"Stan' back!" said Terry to the man.

"That's no way to *pr*oceed. Here! all o' ye come out!"

The men obeyed sullenly and reluctantly.

"Now," said Terry to one of them, "now she'll go. Push away!"

The man obeyed, but in his flurry pushed too hard, lost his grip of the boat, and toppled into the water. Terry caught him by the collar and hauled him out.

"That'll cool yir heels," he said, "ye clumsy coward, ye! Now, how are we to get across?"

By this time the rest of the Squad were safely in Bilboa. Terry walked down to the bank and cried to them: "Hillo there! Go an' catch that boat."

"Divil a fut then," answered Barney Dolan; "go an' catch her yirself."

"Yir a parcel o' damned cowards," Terry said across the water. "First ye run away an' then ye desert yir comrades. Bah!"

"We ran away together then, Terry avick," said Barney; "shure it's a soldier's juty to folly his l'ader."

"Bah!" said Terry in disgust. "Yi're a holy rabble."

Then Mr. Dooley came to Terry's side and called:

"Och! boys, boys, don't lave us! Come for us, boys! Och, do!"

"Is that yirself, Misther Dooley?" said Barney, who, being safe, was willing to play the torturer. "Arrah, where's yir modesty, Misther Dooley? Is it ax common people lek uz to do ye sarvice yi'd do? Och, Misther Dooley!"

Then Mr. Farrell spoke.

"Barney Dolan," he said, "quit your noise. Don't be a bigger coward nor you are. You're safe now an' can bleather. Micky Dolan, remember your oath an' sen' that cot over quick."

"I'm comin', Mr. Farrell," said Micky, and at once he and Shan Grogan shoved off. They caught the lost boat, brought her to land, took Mr. Dooley and Mr. Farrell and Terry Fitch aboard, and landed them safely on their native shore.

"Oh, thank God, thank God!" said Mr. Dooley as he reached land: "The fright I've had this night!"

"Yes," said Terry Fitch with the voice of the scorner, "an' only for the fright in *your* bloated oul carcass we'd ha' seen sights an' heerd tales this blessed night. Go home an' hang yirself!"

So saying Terry put his cane under his arm and walked off. But Mr. Farrell ran after him and caught him by the collar.

"Terry," he said, "don't be foolish. Remember your oath an' forget yourself! Sleep on your words afore ye say much."

"Let me go!" Terry said.

Mr. Farrell faced him and caught him by both arms. "Terry," said he, "do as I bid ye. Mind, no wan seen *uz! We* know all. Howld your tongue. D'ye hear!"

"All right," said Terry, and went off.

Then Mr. Farrell went back to Mr. Dooley.

"Come, President!" he said, "don't set a bad example. You're safe now, man alive! Come away home with me an' have a drop to steady ye."

"Ay, ay! Mr. Farrell," said the President, "what ye say's true. Mebbe home is the best place, an' mebbe a wee drop widn't hurt."

And with that the two linked arms and set off through the fields, Mr. Farrell talking fluent comfort as he went.

Shan Grogan and Micky Dolan pulled up their cot and locked her by the chain to a tree. Then they took the oars and paddle and turned their faces homewards. Their way lay aslant the hill that faced Rhamus.

"Well, Shan?" said Micky.

"Ay, Micky!" said Shan.

Both walked on a bit, then Micky threw down his share of the burden and took out his pipe.

"Me heart's jumpin' yit," he said. "Mebbe a draw 'd do me gwid."

"Ay, faith," said Shan, and did likewise. They sat down on the oars and leisurely puffed.

Right before them Rhamus Castle stood grim and solid against the sky. Below was the river like a silver streak in the moonlight. Both men were filled with a blessed sense of relief. They eyed the scene of their flight, and unfeignedly thanked the blessed Saints for their safe deliverance. Never before had their hearts so warmed to the sod of their native Bilboa. The very hedges about them bent towards them in welcome protection. Micky put his chin on his hand, took a great puff, and sighed.

"Well, Micky?" said Shan.

"Ay, lad!" said Micky.

"We're well out o' *yon*," said Shan.

"We are that," said Micky.

Then both smoked on. After a while Micky rose and stretched himself.

"Mebbe we'd better be movin', Shan," he said. "It must be late."

"Ay, faith, mebbe we'd better," Shan answered. "I'm keepin' the dure open."

Visions of Biddy at home quickened his actions and dulled his sense of happiness. They shouldered the oars and paddle and started again up the hill. Presently they took to a lane and went down towards Leemore Lough. At the foot of the hill Micky gave up his oar and paddle to Shan.

"Good-night, Shan," he said, "an' pleasant drames to ye."

"Good-night, Micky," Shan replied, "an' the same to you."

Then Micky turned off through a gate to his house, and Shan walked on down the lane. He had gone about twenty yards when a voice came through the hedge on his left.

"Shan!" it said.

He started and dropped his load.

"Shan," the voice said again, "it's only me!"

"Who? Micky?"

"Yis."

"Och! bad luck to ye then, what ails ye? Och, the heart's leapin' in me!"

"Whisht!" Micky said. "I only turned to tell ye to be careful what ye say to Biddy."

Shan picked up the oars and paddle.

"All right, Micky," he said. "Thank ye for nothin'! I think I can keep me own counsel."

"Aisy, Shan," said Micky, "no offince where none is meant."

"Aw not at all," said Shan; "but all the same yi've wasted breath."

He walked on for about a quarter of a mile till he came close to Leemore Lough: then he turned down a path home. Leaving his load in the turf-house he went cautiously and looked through the kitchen window.

"Damn!" he muttered, and lifting the latch went in.

Biddy was sitting by the meal chest, opposite the door, patching a pair of corduroy trousers. The fire was out; only a heap of white ashes lay on the hearth showing where the live coals for the morning's kindling were smouldering. A single candle on the chest at Biddy's back struggled feebly with the darkness.

Shan bolted the door, threw his hat on a chair, walked across to a stool by the hearth-stone, and sitting down began to unlace his boots. He took one off, pulled the sock from his toe, and reached for a saucer of grease that stood in a niche in the chimney-nook. Taking a bit of fat on his finger he rubbed it carefully into the leather, then wiped the boot vigorously with a woollen rag. He finished one boot and put it in the chimney corner. As he stooped to untie the other Biddy spoke.

"What kin' 's the night, Shan?" she asked.

"Purty middlin'," replied Shan; "nather here nor there."

He pulled the boot off and fixed it on his hand.

"Yi're late, Shan?" Biddy said.

"Ay, troth, mebbe I am," said Shan. "I thought yi'd be in bed."

Biddy put the trousers on her lap and bit the end of a piece of thread.

"Av coorse ye did," she said, as she turned the eye of her needle towards the light and shot at it with the thread; "av coorse ye did, Shan; I know that well."

There was a minute's silence, during which Biddy threaded her needle and began again on her task, and Shan got as far as the rag on his second boot.

"What kep' ye, Shan, may I ax?" said Biddy, putting the trousers on her knee and smoothing the patch with her hand.

Shan set the boot beside its fellow, then rose and made for the ladder-stairs. Biddy lifted her head and looked at him for the first time.

"Shan!" she said.

"What?" said Shan, turning towards her in the middle of the floor.

"Did ye hear me ax a question?"

"I'm sleepy," said Shan.

"Ye shud be in bed, then."

"I'm goin'."

"Not till ye answer me first," said Biddy.

"Well?" said Shan.

"Ye heerd me," said Biddy.

Shan scratched his head; then made a sudden dash for the stairs. But Biddy was too quick for him and caught him by the coat-tails as he was on the fourth step.

"Come down wid ye," she cried. "Sorra wink ye sleep this night till ye answer me."

She hauled him down and across the floor to the stool by the hearth.

"Now sit there," she said, "till ye spake."

Shan shifted his stool till his back was against the chimney-jamb, then put his head back and pretended to sleep. Biddy worked on, finished one patch, and began another. Shan watched her through his lashes—her face was firm, her lips tight, her whole bearing patiently inflexible. He saw his ruse was a failure and his chances of sleep small. He leaned forward on his stool.

"What is it ye want to know, Biddy?" he asked.

"Ye know."

"I don't."

"Ye do."

"Then I can't answer."

Biddy put down her work.

"Shan," said she, "don't try foolin' me. Ye tried before an' failed, me dear. If ye had nothin' to hide yi'd spake at wanst. For the last time—Where wur ye the night?"

Shan put out his hands.

"Och, Biddy," he said, "shure I can't tell."

"Why not?"

"I can't."

"That's no r'ason."

He put his head on his hands for a while, then looked up.

"Biddy," he said, "cud I trust ye?"

"Ye know best."

"Will ye swear to me not to tell?"

"Tell what?"

"What ye ax me to tell."

"Who cud I tell?"

"Come, Biddy, answer!" said Shan. She shut her mouth firmer than ever and turned the proposal over in her mind. Her curiosity at last got the better of her firmness.

"Well, then," she said, "ye can trust me, Shan."

But her hesitation had given Shan also time to reflect. What was this he was doing? Betraying the Squad! Breaking his oath! Proving himself unworthy of the trust reposed in him as a patriot, a man, and a member of the Committee! His manhood returned to him.

"I'd trust ye as far as I'd throw a bull be the tail," he said to his wife. "Divil a syllable more yi'll get out o' me!"

He rose and stood on the hearthstone looking across at the plates and tins on the dresser. Biddy looked up at him, and seeing his face knew that her chances for that night were gone. She folded her work and put it on the chest. Suddenly her disappointment flared out.

"Shan Grogan," she said, standing before him, the fire rising swiftly to her eyes, "d'ye know who I am? D'ye know what ye mane when ye refuse to answer *me?*"—she struck her fist into her hand—"D'ye think *I'm* to be put off lek this?"

Shan looked her straight in the eyes.

"Biddy, agra," he said solemnly, "don't be a lunytic! I was doin' nothin' wrong the night. Woman alive! isn't the worl' full o' secrets? An' trust the wemen to have their share!"

With that he walked across to the stairs, and, Biddy following, went up to bed.

IV

Shan and Biddy had no family. They lived on a farm that was productive of little but rushes and a crop of poor potatoes. They had two cows, two pigs, a flock of hens and ducks, and a goat to give milk for their tea when the cows went dry. Work as they might, and neither was lazy, they only just managed to keep the thatch over their heads and the pot boiling. Money with them meant the rent and a trifle to fill the basket on odd market days. Their food was potatoes, Indian-meal porridge, and soda-bread and tea. On Sundays, maybe, they had a bit of bacon with their kale, but if so the grease had to last through the week as kitchen for the potatoes. Yet they were better off than their neighbours—the Twenty-five among them—for the squalls of hungry children were never in their ears. To get through the year was their object in life, and to make the time pass smoothly Biddy gossiped and Shan indulged in politics. In their several pleasures they were unrivalled.

The day after the drill was Sunday. Shan shaved, put on a clean shirt, white corduroys, tweed coat and vest, greased boots, and soft felt hat; Biddy rigged herself in a brown winsey dress, black shawl, straw bonnet; and both started for mass. As they walked Shan pondered and Biddy schemed. From their house to the chapel gates, a distance of two miles Irish, neither spoke. They would not have spoken had the way been twice as long.

In the chapel yard, and outside the gates, was a great crowd of intending worshippers. The men in groups of threes and fours were discussing the weather, the crops, the latest news; the women, in smaller groups, shook their heads and wagged their tongues over their hopes and their joys, their trials and tribulations. Mr. Dooley was there, still looking slightly perturbed, as he would say, but quite aware of his importance and superior appearance among so many vulgar people. Mr. Farrell was there, straight and active and neatly dressed, with just a shade of worry on his brow, and his eyes a little more restless. Terry Fitch was leaning against the chapel wall joking with some of the boys. And there was Micky Dolan talking to James O'Gara and Phil Brady—all in clean clothes and looking much as usual. The rest of the Twenty-five, wearing brave faces for all their late adventures, were scattered here and there among the groups.

Shan hooked his thumb in his button-hole, and Biddy dropped the tail of her dress, as they came within sight of the chapel. Putting on smiling faces, they gave the time of day in cheerful tones to all of their acquaintance as they passed through the knots of lads and lasses, and between the talking groups, that took up the grass on each side of the road. At the gate they parted company, Shan carelessly making for Micky Dolan's group, and Biddy stopping short to talk with Mrs. Cafferty.

"An' how's yirself this blessed mornin', Mrs. Cafferty?" said Biddy, as she lifted her tail from the dust and crossed her hands before her.

"Och, donny enough, Mrs. Grogan, donny enough," said Mrs. Cafferty; "an' how's yirself?"

"Well, purty middlin', I thank the Lord," said Biddy, "I musn't complain. I might be worse an' I cud be better."

"Ay, indeed," replied Mrs. Cafferty, "ay, indeed! It's truth yi're tellin'."

"How's all at home?" asked Biddy.

"Och, purty fair now," said Mrs. Cafferty; "father's poorly, an' the childer have a power o' coulds—but, thank the Lord! I can't complain."

"How's the gwid man himself?" asked Biddy.

"Well now, he stan's it rightly," said Mrs. Cafferty, "stan's it first rate, so he does."

"I don't see him about," said Biddy.

"Well, he's over yonder be the dure talkin' to James Hogan," said Mrs. Cafferty.

Both women sent their eyes the round of the groups.

"*Your* man luks right well, Mrs. Grogan, so he does," said Mrs. Cafferty, turning her eyes to where Shan and his companions were holding very confidential talk. Biddy also looked and her lips closed. Secrets! she thought; oh! these men and their secrets.

"Faith now, him an' th' others are havin' a mighty close chat," went on Mrs. Cafferty—"mighty close!"

"Ay," said Biddy, "so they are. Widn't ye lek to know what they're confabbin' about?"

"Troth, an' I jist wid," said Mrs. Cafferty, "for its divils the men are, anyway."

Biddy looked at Mrs. Cafferty swiftly.

"Yi're right there," said she: "what's *he* been doin'?"

"Och, sorra much now," said Mrs. Cafferty, "nothin' more'n ordinary."

"H'm," said Biddy; "an' ye notice nothin' *av late?*"

"Och, no," said Mrs. Cafferty; "n' more than usual."

"Well now," said Biddy, "that's gwid!—that's gwid! Mebbe he stops out late now?"

"Mebbe," said Mrs. Cafferty; "mebbe. But I haven't noticed. Shure min *will* kaley!"

"Was he out late last night?" asked Biddy.

"Oh ay," said Mrs. Cafferty; " 'deed he was. But no later than ordinary; aw no!"

"Was he all right when he did come?" asked Biddy.

"Well, to tell God's truth," said Mrs. Cafferty, "he luk't a trifle scart."

"Ha!" said Biddy. "Was it poteen ye think?"

"Och, no; he was as sober as a jedge."

"Dear, dear, dear!" said Biddy. "An' what d'ye call late, now?"

The time agreed almost with that at which Shan had appeared.

Biddy looked once more at Shan. His finger was up and his head wagging from side to side to catch the ears of the group.

Then Biddy dropped her skirt and leaned towards Mrs. Cafferty.

"I say, Mary," she said, "there's somethin' up."

And with a very grave face and a wealth of speech Biddy confided to Mary her suspicions.

Meanwhile Shan was holding forth on the powers of committees.

The question was, What now about the drills? They all knew now that *th' others* were preparing. They knew also that the preparation was widespread. Sergeant Mires had called a roll in Rhamus Castle that swept a country-side. Every man in the

Eighteen was as well known to every man in the Twenty-five as the Twenty-five were to each other. Further, *th' others* had been drilling for some time, as their movements showed. Should these facts influence them? Only to spur them on, said Shan. They knew now what was only guessed before, and the very reason they had started drilling was only justified. The group nodded assent to this conclusion. Next, Would the Squad turn up? Micky Dolan doubted; James O'Gara was sure some of them would; Phil Brady declared that he wouldn't so long as Terry Fitch was drill-master. Shan said that they had determined, in meeting assembled, to prepare. Would it become them then as men to draw back? No, he said, it would not. Further, he declared it was the Committee's duty, and was within its power, to make every man fulfil his compact in this matter. Here the group joined issue. Phil Brady flatly denied the alleged power of the Committee. He said its members were no better than the rest, and could only act at the bidding of the Squad. Shan retorted that the Committee was "indipindint of the Squad—teetotally indipindint."

"How's that?" asked James O'Gara. "I'm a mimber meself, but I'm also wan av the Squad."

"That's so," said Micky Dolan. "The same here."

"What I mane is this," said Shan. "The Commit*tee*'s given powers by the Squad to act for it, an' what it sez is to be done."

"I heerd nothin' about that at the meetin'," Phil Brady said.

"Man!" said Shan, "don't ye know nothin'? Av coorse ye didn't! But don't ye know the *nature* av a Commit*tee*?"

"Well enough," said Phil.

"Don't ye know that a Commit*tee*'s a Commit*tee* all the worl' over?" said Shan. "The powers av a Commit*tee* are laid down in black an' white. What *wan* does th' other can do."

"Who towld ye that?" asked Phil.

"Why, man alive!" Shan cried, "iverywan knows that! Don't ye read the papers? Did ye niver hear av the House av Commons? What does a Committee av *it* do? Why, alters Bills wholesale, an' what *it* sez becomes law."

"That's so," said Micky Dolan. "Begorra I'm thinkin' yi're right, Shan."

"Av coorse," said Shan, "it's only common knowledge."

"Well," said Phil, "supposin' now that the three o' ye there bein' committee men towld me to drill an' I refused. What'd happen?"

"The three av uz cudn't," said Shan. "There'd have to be a majority at laste."

"Well, supposin' yis all agreed an' I refused?"

This was a poser.

"Well," said Micky Dolan, turning a blank look at the chapel-wall, "that'd be atween yirself an' yir Maker, Phil."

This gave Shan his cue.

"Phil," said he solemnly, "yi're in a stubborn humour this day, an' what yi're sayin' isn't what ye mane. Ax yirself on yir knees afore ye go home what yir juty 'd be. Man! this is no personal matter; it's higher interests than our dirty carcasses, Phil, that's at stake."

Just then a movement began towards the chapel, and with bended heads Shan and his companions joined the throng and went in to worship.

Micky Dolan and Shan Grogan walked home together, Mrs. Dolan and Biddy bringing up the rear. Biddy had done a good morning's work. She had heard a little, guessed a great deal, and had dropped here and there a knowing hint or two for the benefit of a neighbour. Already she was firmly convinced that all the men in Bilboa were plotting with some wicked and unlawful intent. Wasn't it plain? Couldn't a blind man see it? Couldn't

Mrs. Dolan herself see it? Shure it was plain as a pike-staff, said Biddy, well knowing that every word she said would soon compass Bilboa.

Shan and Micky walked, for the most part, one each side of the road and fired their conversation across the dust. But occasionally they would run together and, first casting a glance over their shoulders at the women, converse for a little on the topic that was next their heart. During one of these meetings, Micky whispered to Shan a message from Mr. Farrell to the effect that the Committee was to meet that evening at eight o'clock in O'Gara's barn. Then they swerved off the grass, and Shan turned the news over in his mind. What perplexed him was, how was he to evade Biddy and how excuse his absence? He walked for a good while without speaking, then raised his head and made for the middle of the road.

"Ye mind last night," he whispered to Micky; "well, I had the divil's own trial wid Biddy."

"I thought ye wid," said Micky. "I know what women are meself."

"Well, most av uz do," said Shan.

"An' how did ye manage?" asked Micky.

" 'Twas sore," said Shan.

"An' ye towld?"

"Is it lek'ly?" asked Shan, with a fine show of scorn. "Knowin' the kin' o' man I am, d'ye think it lek'ly?"

"Well," said Micky, with a grin, "troth I was afeerd. Knowin' what I do, I'd give ye a power av excuse."

"Ay," said Shan. "Oh, ay!"

Then they swerved to the grass for a while.

"I'm wonderin', Micky," said Shan as his shoulder touched Micky's, "how I'll manage to slope off the night."

"Are ye now?" asked Micky.

"I'm afeerd," said Shan, pursing his mouth, "it'll be hard."

"Ay, ay," said Micky; and they took to the grass again.

When they were within sight of Shan's house they met for the last time.

"I've been turnin' things over in me min'," said Shan, "an' things look doubtful. It's a risky business."

"It is so," assented Micky.

"Will ye be Farrell's way after dinnertime?" Shan asked.

"Mebbe I might," said Micky; "sure I cud make it me business."

"Well, if ye see him, say that mebbe we'd better ha' time to think things over afore we meet," said Shan. "Wednesday 'd suit better, I think; an' mebbe we'd better say an earlier hour—three or four o'clock, say. An' say that as gwid a place to meet as any 'd be the bushy fort in Johnstone's big meadow along the river. I cud make an excuse to go there. Eh?"

"I'll go," said Micky. "I'd do more'n that to pull a friend out av a hole."

By this the two had reached the path leading to Shan's house, and there, in innocent talk about the crops, they waited for their footsore and hungry wives.

V

The Eighteen, in their flight from Rhamus, finding they were not pursued, checked themselves before they reached the road and, in the shade of a hedge, held counsel. Opinions differed as to who or what frightened them. One suggested spies; another, some of the boys playing tricks; another, stones falling from the wall; another, ghosts. All were agreed, however, that the cause, be it what it might, was something strange, sudden, and "powerful."

"I thought the judgment day had come," said Robert Young; "me heart stud still expectin' the trumpet av Gabriel."

"The wall luk'd alive wid divils' imps," said William Sherson; "I seen the forms av them dancin' in the ivy."

"Mebbe 'twas only a whirl-blast shakin' the branches," suggested John McGarvey.

"An' how does that account for the feet thumpin' on the grass an' the yellin' an' scramblin'?" asked Ned Noble. "They were men as shure as gun 's iron. Yon clatter was made be flesh an' blood."

"You wur facing the wall, Sergeant," said Henry Marvin; "you shud 'a seen somethin' plain."

"I heer'd a powerful t'arin' in the ivy," said Sergeant Mires; "an' then a yell. Then the top o' the wall grew alive, an' I heerd the sound o' leapin' an' fallin'—that's all."

"Well," said Robert Young, "it's over an' gone, an' here we are. Mebbe we'd better cut?"

"Mebbe we'd better," said two or three.

"Shure there's no gwid yelpin' over spilt milk," said Ned Noble. "I say—slope."

"I propose, before we go," said Sergeant Mires, "to ease our min's, that a couple of us go back an' have a look roun'. I'll go for one. Who'll come?"

No one volunteered. Is it risk their skins again? thought the Eighteen. Not they. The Sergeant might if he liked; he was old and foolish—but they? Well, no!

"What! no one'll come?" said the Sergeant. "Well, then, I'll go meself. You'll stay till I come back?"

"Oh, ay," said the Squad, "we'll wait; av coorse."

Then Sergeant Mires took off his shako and, bending low, jouked along the hedge up the hill. The Squad watched him anxiously, holding their breath almost till they saw his red and white figure clamber through the hole in the castle-wall. It was fifteen minutes before the Sergeant came back, dressed in his ordinary clothes and carrying his carpet bag. The Squad had begun to grow anxious; now they were reassured: one by one the pipes came from the waistcoat pockets and were lit.

"Be me sowl, Sergeant," said Ned Noble, giving his neighbour a knowing dig with his elbow, "but ye had gwid r'ason to go back. It's the sorry figure you'd ha' cut along the road in yir regimentals. Faith, the dogs 'd 'a' had fun!"

The Sergeant carefully put his bag against the ditch.

"Whisht, Ned," he said, "it's no time for vain jestin'. Boys, 'twas men wur yonder. I went over the ground carefully, an' the marks o' boots are plain to be seen on the grass, an' the ivy on the walls is all broken an' bent. There's clear marks av a scramble on the ditch-bank, an' the groun's all tore up where they jumped from it."

"Who the divil *cud* it be?" said the Eighteen.

"We've talked all that over before," said the Sergeant; "an' we may talk all night and get no further. I propose we go home now an' sleep on it. But let me warn ye, men, not to let your tongues get the better o' you over this affair. Laste said soonest mended, as the sayin' is. Let all o' ye that leks come to Gorteen, Monday night at the usual hour. Now, go home steady, men."

Then by ones and twos, and with much caution, the Eighteen took to the road and gravely went to their homes.

Gorteen was the name of the townland where Samuel Mires lived. His farm of thirty acres was one of the best in the country; his house was the talk of the neighbourhood. It stood halfway up a hill, a little back from the road, and shone in its whiteness behind creepers and flowers and roses. You reached the door through a garden, where everything bloomed its old-fashioned best in the most perfect order. Behind were apple-trees and pear-trees, plum-trees and cherry-trees; and to the left, among the parsnips, carrots, and onions, were the currant and gooseberry bushes. The house was long and low, with the thatch low on the eaves, and the doors and windows painted white and green. If you were only an ordinary visitor you never thought of intruding on the front garden, but took to the lane which wound round the haggard, and followed it, past the churning-machine, into the backyard, where the ducks and hens were, and where the offices were as clean and white and well-thatched as hands could make them. Such was Samuel's home at its best; at its worst it only lacked the beauty of the flowers and the glory of summer.

It was down the lane that the Eighteen went on the Monday night following the drill. They sauntered between the trim hedges in a very careless way, passed through the yard, and mounted the ladder that led to the door of the loft over the byre. There they found tables and chairs, and candles in bright brass candlesticks. In a corner of the loft was a big drum with its hoops painted orange and blue. Standing by its was a furled flag tied round with a piece of orange ribbon. Hanging on the wall were two drumsticks; and underneath them stood a black box, on which in white were the letters "G. L. O. L." This was the head-quarters of the Gorteen Loyal Orange Lodge. The Eighteen were therefore as safe as at home.

They seated themselves, lit their pipes, and began to talk. There was no attempt made to form a meeting, nor was there anyone in authority. Equality was the motto of the assemblage. Here one man was as good as another—as good a man, patriot, or scholar. Here Sergeant Mires was plain Samuel, whatever he might be elsewhere; a good man, to be sure, and a good farmer, but, in the eyes of his neighbours, "only plain stirabout like themselves."

"Well, men," he said, as he sat down after bolting the door, "any news?"

Robert Young shifted his left leg over his right and said: "Well, I've heerd none."

"That's big news," said Ned Noble, "*an*' most satisfyin'."

"Well now," said Henry Marvin, in his wisest tones, "you know the oul' sayin', 'No news is the best news.'"

"Is that so now, Henry?" said Ned. "Well, well, the wonders o' this worl'!"

The Eighteen took out their pipes and wiped their mouths over the pleasantry.

"Well now, Henry," went on Ned, "tell uz, confidential lek, what kin's yir own news?"

"It's av the best," said Henry; "it's worth nothin'—lek yirself."

The pipes came out again, and the Eighteen shifted their chairs delightedly.

Ned turned his chair that he might face Henry. He had his reputation as a witty man to uphold.

"Henry," said Ned, "what's that ye made bould to say?"

"Ye heerd," said Henry.

"Did ye make free to remark that I was worth nothin'?"

"I did," said Henry.

"Then," said Ned, leaning back in his chair with his thumbs in the arm-holes of his waistcoat, "before the company, prove yir words."

"It's aisly done," said Henry.

"All the better for you," said Ned.

"Well, yi're wastin' time be tryin' to gag a better man nor yirself, for one thing," said Henry; "an', for another, the breed o' ye niver was good for much."

The Eighteen fell back in their chairs and drew their breath sharply between their teeth. Then they shut their lips, and gravely nodded each towards his neighbour.

Ned squared himself before Henry and glared at the daring man.

"What's that ye say, ye—ye puckin, ye?" he shouted. "Is it the lek o' you that's talkin' about breed—you that was brought up on a doughall (dunghill)? Ye needle-nosed canat, ye! Prove yir words, sur, prove them, I say, or be the Holy I'll bang ye black an' blue."

Henry coolly crossed his legs and folded his arms.

"Don't stop till yi're tired, acushla," he said; "hard words brek no bones, as the sayin' is, an' prove nothin'. I'm sure the company 'll be glad to hear more o' ye."

Ned looked at him for a little, then turned round his chair with a rush.

"Och," he said, scornfully, "shure I widn't lower meself to argy wid the lek o' you."

"So be it," said Henry. "I'll be all the sweeter for it." So saying, he filled his pipe again, and for the rest of the evening wore the smile of the conqueror.

This mighty conflict of wits over, the Eighteen settled themselves to serious discussion. Was there any news? Samuel Mires asked once more. No one had heard anything. Had any one formed an opinion about the late affair? he suggested. The opinions of all the Eighteen agreed—Firstly, that the late affair was mysterious; secondly, that it was unexpected; thirdly, that it should be investigated. Next, the question arose: How should it be investigated? To this there could be found no reply till the supreme point was decided: Should there be any more drills?

Samuel Mires' answer to this was emphatic. Most decidedly there should be. "'No man,'" he quoted, "'having put his hand to the plough, and looking back, is fit for the Kingdom of Heaven.'"

"There's no question o' Heaven here," said Ned Noble; "an', so far as I can see, there's no call on any av uz to risk our skins."

"We mustn't think of ourselves at all," replied Samuel; "our principles are at stake."

"Principles are all very well," said Ned, "but life is sweet."

"I ask this question," said Samuel, "with all seriousness: Would life be sweet under a Fenian Parliament?"

The Eighteen pondered this with solemn faces. No, they decided, life would be hell on earth.

"Then," said Samuel, "our duty's clear as the day."

"What I say is this," said Ned Noble, emphasising his words with bangs on the table, "we'd be fools to risk our lives for what may niver be."

"We'd be greater fools," said Samuel Mires, "to sit lek childer an' wait for what is likely to be."

"Ay, but people say," said Robert Young, "that we've nothin' to fear."

"Nothin' to fear!" said Samuel Mires. "I ax all o' ye to search your hearts an' see if that's true. Luk at the past. Luk at the present. D'ye think if *they* get the chance, they won't try to crush us. Man! They're just waitin' to spit in our faces. They're just dyin' to strangle us an' our religion. Men," went on the Sergeant, "look at that flag! Wid ye like to see it torn and disgraced? Are ye goin' to forget the memory o' William the Third, what he fought for an' what he gev us? Sure, we have need to be well ashamed!"

A wave of emotion passed over the Eighteen; the spirit of Faction fell upon them; with one voice they declared their loyalty to their colours, and their detestation of "Pope and Popery, brass money, and wooden shoes." Thus their souls glowed within them, and they sat in happy brotherhood.

It was Henry Marvin who broke the spell.

"After all," he said, "there's much cry over little wool, as they say. Mebbe, after all, they were frien's that frightened uz on Saterday."

"Faith, that's so," said the Eighteen; "mebbe they wur."

"Anyway, whoever they wur ran away," said Henry, "an' didn't hurt uz."

"Faith, that's truth," said the Eighteen.

"Furthermore," said Henry, "it doesn't belong to *uz* to stop the drills. A general meetin' must decide that question."

"Hear, hear," said the Eighteen. "Bedad, Henry, that's correct."

"It's our juty, then," said Henry, "to lay our infermation before a general meetin'."

"Just that," assented the Eighteen.

"*But*, as the sayin' is," Henry continued, "we shid luk afore we le'p; an', that bein' so, I think we shid try to lay infermation that's correct afore the meetin'."

"Hear, hear," said the Eighteen.

"How's that to be done?" asked Henry, leaning forward and eyeing the assembly.

There was a minute's hard thought that brought forth no suggestion.

"Then here ye are," said Henry, emphasising his words by tapping his pipe-stem on his palm; "let some av uz go as usual to Rhamus nex' Saterday an' lie in wait outside. Then we can see what we can see."

He leaned back in his chair with a knowing look. Ned Noble turned towards him.

"Bedad, Henry," he said, "yi 're in fettle the night. Give uz yi 're bone."

The two solemnly shook hands.

"Friends still?" asked Ned.

"True blue, brother," replied Henry. And the rift in the lute closed.

Then the Eighteen approved Henry's suggestion, and drew lots to see who should go. The lots fell on Joseph Donaldson, John Martin, Henry Marvin, Richard Hoey, Henry Bredin, and Ned Noble.

"I think that's all," said Samuel Mires. "Av coorse, what has passed is only among ourselves. We can say nothin' to anyone before the general meetin'."

He rose to go, but Ned Noble waved him down.

"Sit down, Sergeant," he said, "it's meet that this meetin' brek up wid harmony."

And expanding his great chest, Ned roared out his favourite song, of which the refrain runs—

> *"For we're the Boys that fear no noise,*
> *An' niver will sur-rendur."*

VI

The following Wednesday, after dinner, Shan Grogan took down his fishing-rods from the rafters of the turf-house, made a great pretence of mending their tackle before Biddy, and then told her he was going to try his luck at fishing.

"Where did ye think o' tryin'?" Biddy asked.

"Och, mebbe at the stakes in the river," Shan answered.

"Ha' ye fed?" Biddy asked.

"Och, no," said Shan; "but what odds? The fish 'll bite this fine weather widout feedin'. Anyway, shure it's only to wile away an hour or so."

"Yi'd be better employed spreadin' the turf," said Biddy, "this fine day."

"Aw, they're hardly fit; an' what's the hurry, anyway?" said Shan.

"Ivery hurry, Shan," said Biddy. "How long 'll ye be?"

"Aw, I'll be back be tay-time," he said. "Shure if I don't, an hour more or less is nather here nor there."

He shouldered his rods and was marching off down the fields when Biddy called—

"Where's your worms, Shan?"

Shan threw down his rods and went back.

"Faith, me wits is wool-gatherin'," he said, as he passed Biddy to get a spade from the byre. "Get uz an' owl' porringer, Biddy."

As he came back, Biddy met him on the street with an old rusty porringer in her hand.

"Luk me in the face, Shan," she said; "where are ye goin' to?"

"Haven't I towld ye, woman!" he answered testily. "Isn't wanst enough?"

He took the porringer, and with the spade on his shoulder went to dig worms in the haggard.

"Och, Shan, Shan!" Biddy said after him. "Och, Shan, Shan!"

Presently he came back with the spade, put it in the byre, then trudged down the field to his rods, picked them up, and made for the cot on the lake.

Biddy from the door watched him bale the cot, fix the seats, unlock the oars, push the cot out, then slowly pull down the lake.

She shook her head at him. "Och, Shan, Shan!" she said.

Then she locked the door and crossed the hill till she had the river in view. She saw Shan row on, pass the fishing-stakes, and finally land opposite the bushy fort in Mr. Johnstone's big meadow. He pulled the cot up, and soon disappeared into the fort. Presently another cot came up the river, having one man rowing and another paddling. These also landed in Johnstone's meadow and went to the fort.

"Och, Shan, Shan!" Biddy said, as she turned homewards. "Och, Shan, Shan!"

Half-an-hour afterwards she and Mrs. Cafferty were exchanging ideas that soon were common property among many women in Bilboa.

Meanwhile the Committee was sitting in the fort. The place was a circular mound, fringed with trees and scrubby whitethorns. Inside the fringe was flat and grassy, and dotted with big mossy stones. On these sat the Committee in meeting assembled under the blue vault of heaven.

The first question was, Should the drills be continued? Yes, replied the Committee, not answering heedlessly, but with the show of importance that became a public body elected to perform responsible and onerous duties.

Next was advanced, Would the Squad turn out to drill? This involved the rights and powers of committees, and gave Shan his chance. He waxed eloquent in their defence; cited examples and precedents; answered objections and criticisms—all in a flame of enthusiasm, his hands flashing about, his eyes ceaselessly going the round of his audience.

"But," said Micky Dolan, when Shan's tongue ceased, "when all's said, there's still Phil Brady's view. All the committees this side o' purgatory won't make an' onwillin' man do what he's no min' to."

"The Committee o' the British Parlemint," said Shan, "cud sen' its own members up stairs to the clock tower; it cud—"

"Whisht!" said Mr. Farrell, "don't name the British Parliament here! Ye talk about onwillin'ness—*who's* onwillin'?"

"Some are, I know," said Micky Dolan.

"Who?" asked Mr. Farrell.

"I name no names," said Micky, "but I spake truth."

"Then I don't believe the truth," said Mr. Farrell; "what in blazes makes them onwillin'?"

"That's their own affair," said Micky. "I dunno."

"Ye do know," said Mr. Farrell, "an' won't say! Here! let me know who I'm spakin' to. Mr. Dooley, will you attend drill in future?"

"Well," said Mr. Dooley looking at the sky, "I've no objection, provided violent interruptions, such as we know of, are not forthcomin'."

"In other words," said Mr. Farrell, "you'd like to go to heaven in a han' basket. Very good. An' you now, James O'Gara?"

"I'm willin'," said James.

"An' you, Micky Dolan?"

"I won't say *yit*," said Micky. "If so be that the drills keep on, no doubt I'll go."

"Bah!" said Mr. Farrell. "Spake, Micky Reilly."

"I'll do me juty as a commit*tee* man," said Micky.

"I needn't ax you, I know, Shan Grogan, after all you've said."

Shan shifted on his seat.

"Well," he answered, "so far as I'm concarned I'll try to do me juty. But"—he pursed his lips at thought of Biddy—"there's more'n meself concarned. Mr. Farrell, yi 're a single man an' don't know the tricks av wemen. Pray the Lord ye niver do! But some av them 's powerful quare." Shan puckered up his mouth and waggled his head.

"Ay, ay!" broke in Micky Dolan, "so they are."

"What's all this?" asked Mr. Farrell. "What the jeuce have the wemen to do with us?"

"Yi 're no marr'ed, man," said Shan; "if ye wur yi'd know."

Mr. Farrell looked round in bewilderment. He could see that every face showed some secret sympathy with Shan. He jumped to his feet.

"What's this?" he asked. "All o' ye spake out! What divils' angel 's among ye?"

"Shan," said Micky Dolan, "you spake."

"Well," said Shan, "it's this way. Sit down Mister Farrell, if ye plaze; I can't spake right wid you lookin' lek that afore me. Yi 're no marr'ed man, Mister Farrell, as I've said afore, an' so don't know what some av uz have to put up with. Aw me! but the ways o' wemen is wonderful!" He put his elbows on his knees and looked hard at a whitethorn bush before him. "Some o' them," he went on, "can sniff a thing afore it happens, an' they're all purty cute; but ye may take it as Gospel that whativer a woman doesn't know isn't worth findin' out. Eh, men?" he said to all except Mr. Farrell.

The four sitting with their elbows on their knees and their hands clasped on their pipes, nodded and grunted approval.

"Well," Shan went on, "there's wan among uz—namin' no names an' tellin' no secrets—that's got a wife who's sharp beyant all belief. She's a gwid woman enough in her way, but gabby an' sharp av the nose. An' she, Mr. Farrell, has her suspicions av what's goin' on."

"Well?" said Mr. Farrell.

"At laste," said Shan, "she has her suspicions that *somethin's* goin' on, an', as wemen will, she's ready to think the worst."

"Well?" said Mr. Farrell again.

"Well, when a woman gets it into her head that her man is doin' somethin' wrong," Shan went on, "whether he is or not makes no differ, she tries first to fin' out what it is, an' failin' that, she makes him smart."

"Well?" said Mr. Farrell impatiently.

"That's how the man I spake of is placed," said Shan; "his wife suspects somethin' is up, axes him plump to tell her, an' av coorse gettin' no answer, threatens him wid all kin's av torments."

"If he's a *man*, as ye say," said Mr. Farrell, "he'll have a quick cure for that."

"Mebbe yi'd tell uz what?" asked Shan.

"Tell her that what he does is nothin' to her, an' failin' that, to go to blazes," replied Mr. Farrell.

The five smiled the smile of the knowing, and Shan replied—

"Aw, Mister Farrell, it's aisy to see yi 're no marr'ed man!"

"And what 'll this *man*, as ye call him, do?" asked Farrell.

"Well," said Shan, "he'll go as far as is safe—if he's wise. But he'll stop in time, an' humour the wife a bit if he wants a roof over his head."

"Och, bleather, bleather!" cried Mr. Farrell. "He's no man at all."

He looked round the Committee again.

"But," said he, "what about one man, even if he is on the committee? Shure you're not all oul' wemen? Shure *all* you're wives aren't lek Sha—lek yon one?"

" 'Deed no," said Micky Reilly, "but wan bad fish 'll spoil a lot. Ye might as well try to stop the moon settin' as stop wemen's clack."

"An' this bitch has been goin' the roun's?" said Farrell. "An' in all Bilboa there's not a sensible woman or a man worth his salt? An' our drills 'll be stopped because o' wemen? Is that it? Be God, if it is, I'll wash me han's av such muck!"

"Easy, easy, Mr. Farrell," said Mr. Dooley. "You're unduly exciting yerself. Your inspiration is runnin' riot——"

"Damn inspiration!" cried Farrell. "Damn the whole crew av ye!"

Mr. Dooley got to his feet.

"I'm not used to such langwidge," he said, "an' I must be excused further intercourse——"

Then did Micky Dolan burst into a great laugh, that soon spread to James Hogan and stopped not till even Mr. Dooley's sides shook, and Mr. Farrell alone sat serious.

"What the blazes!—" Mr. Farrell began, rising swiftly and facing the Committee; then, seeing that his anger would avail nothing, and being, moreover, a politic young man, as suddenly calmed himself, and folding his arms waited for the laughter to cease.

"When you're quite done, boys," he said in a little while, "I'll be glad. Come! this is no laughin' matter; I'm spakin' seriously. But if I'm wrong, correct me."

"Well, sit down, then," said Shan Grogan. "Ye want a wife to cool yir temper, so ye do. All I meant to say was that there bein' difficulties in the way, I'll attend drill as often as I can. More mortal man wid a wife can't do. That's what we all mane, isn't it?"

"Jist so," said the four.

"Well," said Mr. Farrell, "I ax pardon for me temper. But all I have to say is, that if Terry Fitch is short of men because o' their wives, there's small hope for Irelan'. We'll see; in the meantime what's next?"

"Ye spoke o' Terry Fitch jist now," said Micky Dolan; "I'd lek to know meself if Terry's very keen to drill the Squad at all?"

"What's that?" said Mr. Farrell. "Who says he isn't?"

"No wan," said Micky; "I only say I'd lek to know."

"But surely Terry's not afeerd av his wife?" said Farrell.

"Mebbe not," said Micky, "an' mebbe he is. Anyway, he was powerful mad wid uz all th'other night, an' spoke purty sharp to us. Ye mind what Phil Brady said to him?"

"Phat!" said Farrell; "every drill-master bullies a bit."

"Ay, ay," said Micky; "but he needn't ha' been so mighty sharp on uz the first night. Besides, people ha' feelin's; an' Terry cud hear well enough that we were glad Phil spoke up as he did."

"An' forby that," said James O'Gara, who was a man of few words, "he called uz cowards on the river bank."

"An' he called me names," said Mr. Dooley, "and insulted me."

"Oh, boys, boys, quit!" said Mr. Farrell. "Terry's lek another: he has his temper. He's good at bottom, an' he's the best man to be had. Mebbe we'd better all go an' see him after this. A little soft-soap 'll bring him roun'."

"Mind ye," said Micky Dolan, "I'm sayin' nothin' agen Terry Fitch—but his ways may keep men away; an' I was wonderin' how he'd feel himself."

"Well, boys," Mr. Farrell said, rising to his feet, "Terry Fitch is all very good as an excuse; so are the wemen; so is the fear of our dirty hides—but, all bein' said, the man who doesn't put Irelan' before such childer's bleather is a chicken-hearted pishtrogue. We've iverything on our side. No one knew us th' other night; we know what *th' others* are doin'; the flowin' tide is with us; only a parcel of ould wemen, for all their red coats and white britches, is against us; there's iverything before us—an' if we can't take advantage of things, we're fools. That's all! Be heaven, but I think we are! Here we've been blarneyin' for an hour an' a half, and all that's settled is we'll drill if the *wemen* let us, an' if Terry Fitch 'll drill us.—Let's out o' this! I'm sick av it!"

At the river side Shan remembered his telling Biddy he would be home about tea-time.

"What's about the time, Mr. Dooley?" he asked.

It was five o'clock.

"Then, I think," said Shan, "I'll be after scuddin' home. I promised—there's somethin' special I've got to do."

"Away wid ye," said Mr. Farrell; "an' the Lord protect ye, Shan!"

"Begob, then, Shan," said Micky Dolan, "but as yi're goin' my way but I think I'll go wid ye."

"Any more o' ye with wives waitin' on ye?" asked Mr. Farrell. " 'Cause if there is, don't disappoint them. I can tackle Terry Fitch alone."

"I'm goin' wid ye, anyway," said James O'Gara, who was a widower.

"An' I'll go, too," said Micky Reilly, whose wife was in town.

"And I'll chance the consequences," said Mr. Dooley.

Then, amid jeers and skirls, Shan and Micky set off homewards; and the rest of the Committee crowded into a cot and went to seek Terry Fitch.

It was deemed wise that Mr. Farrell—who, seated comfortably, and well suited with a smooth-drawing pipe, soon recovered his good humour—should go to Terry's house alone, the others keeping within easy call. He found Mrs. Fitch in the dirty yard, pounding potatoes in a tub. Her hair was tangled and fell about her face, her big red arms were bare to the armpits, her dress was looped up to her waist, showing a dirty quilted petticoat and grimed feet. A young child stood by the tub crowing at the flying beetle. All about the yard, among the hens and ducks, were children—dear knows how many—dirty, ragged, but happy. One of them saw Mr. Farrell coming, and ran to tell his mother. She dropped her skirt, pushed the hair back from her face, and took up the child.

"Fine day to ye, Mrs. Fitch," said Mr. Farrell; "an' how's yourself?"

"Och, bravely, Mr. Farrell—can't complain, thank God; an' how's yirself?"

"First class, thank ye kindly, Mrs. Fitch; an' how's all your care?"

"Well, now, hearty, thank God, Mr. Farrell," said the mother, looking round her brood.

"Well, God bless them," said Mr. Farrell; "they're a fine parcel o' childer. What's their names, now? Come here, me son, an' tell us your name."

He lifted a fine curly-headed lad, for all his dirt, to his shoulder, and gave him a "shuggy" as the boy called it. Then he gave another a like treat, and another, till all were satisfied. The mother stood smiling with pride, and inwardly blessing Mr. Farrell.

"Well, they're as weighty an' fine a lot of childer, God bless them, as iver I felt," said Mr. Farrell, puffing from his exertion; "ye should be proud o' them, Mrs. Fitch."

"Aw 'deed, I am," said the mother; " 'deed, I am—but they're a sore bother, now, at times."

"Aw, ay," said Mr. Farrell; "shure, there's no pleasure without its pain."

" 'Deed, no," said she; " 'deed it's God's truth."

"An' how's Terry?" asked Mr. Farrell.

"Aw, rightly now; rightly," she said. "He's down in the bog yonder, at the turf—him an' Lizzie an' Paddy."

"Well, now, as I'm this far," said Mr. Farrell, "I think I'll just go an' see him. Terry's a man I've a big respec' for. He an' I get on powerful. Many's the chat we have, faith, an' many's the joke. Make him drop over our way oftener. Well, good day to ye, Mrs. Fitch—you an' your fine childer; God bless them an' you."

"Good day to ye, Mr. Farrell," said Mrs. Fitch; "an' blessin's be wid ye."

Perhaps, had Mr. Farrell gone the rounds of all the houses in Bilboa, he might have made things easier for his Squad. Certainly he won Mrs. Fitch's heart that day—the free, good-hearted young man he was, God bless him!—and further, gave her hope that after all Biddy Grogan's suspicions were only bleather. Hadn't Mr. Farrell said that Terry and he were fast friends, and that Terry sometimes went to see him? Well! And bad as Terry was at times—drunken and brutal—yet Mrs. Fitch was not the one to deny him his pleasure, particularly with such a well-favoured, promising young man as Mr. Farrell. Biddy Grogan might talk, she thought, but after all, maybe 'twas only talk. Fortunately, the bog was out of her view.

Terry, stripped to the shirt and trousers, was down in a bog-hole cutting turf; Paddy, also half naked, was catching the wet peat as it came up from the spade, and Lizzie was wheeling it through the heather, and scattering it in barrow-loads here and there to dry.

"Daddy," said Lizzie, dropping her barrow and running to the bog-hole, "here's four men comin' across the bog."

Terry sunk his foot in the side of the hole, and, leaning on his turf spade, stretched his neck to see.

"Ho, ho!" he said to himself; then to Lizzie, "You an' Paddy run off an' see if the cows are all right. Run away now, till I have a smoke."

Then, taking his spade with him, he got up on the bank and there waited for the Committee.

"Well, well, Terry, to be sure," said Mr. Dooley stopping short, "is this how we find ye? The hardy man ye must be an' the weather none too warm!"

"Better here than drillin' numsculls," said Terry. "Yi're very welcome, gintlemin!"

"Thank ye, Terry," said Mr. Farrell. "We thought we'd just luk ye up."

"As the Committee or as yirselves?"

"Well, as ourselves first an' the Committee afterwards."

"I see," said Terry; "I see. An' what does yirselves want?"

"Well we had to transact some business the day," answered Farrell, "an' we foun' that *your* opinion was necessary."

"I see," said Terry. "Well, I'm listenin'."

"It's about the drills, Terry," said Farrell. "We want your advice about them."

"As the Committee yi're now spakin'?"

"As one man to another."

"Well, spakin' as a man then," said Terry, "to tell truth, me advice is bad."

"What might it be?" asked Farrell.

"For the Committee to drill the Squad themselves."

"We're in earnest, Terry," said Farrell. "We'd lek no foolishness."

"Is it foolishness?" said Terry. "For that same ye can't do better than try to drill unholy ijuts—that run away, too!"

"Ye ran yirself, Terry," said Micky Reilly.

"The man that says that's a liar, Committee man or no Committee man," said Terry. "Prove yir words, Micky Reilly, or——"

"Didn't we all run together," said Micky, "one wid another?"

"Ye all did," said Terry. "That's mortial truth. *I* retr'ated! I *avoided* the inimy for a piece, then I retired studdy an' solid, as ye all seen for yirselves."

"Terry," said Micky, "I'm not prepared to dispute wid ye, an' I ax pardon if I'm wrong."

"I take yir word, Micky," said Terry. "An' what's nex'?"

"Ye say, then, Terry," said Mr. Farrell, "that ye don't feel inclined to take the Squad again?"

"No such a thing," said Terry. "As a *man* I said I thought it was foolishness. Be a man I mane a sojer."

"Well then, spakin' as one of ourselves?"

"I say try again."

"Tight fella, Terry!" said James O'Gara. "Me brave gossoon!"

"Provided," Terry went on, taking his spade from his shoulder and driving the blade into the turf between his bare feet—"pro-vided I'm given a guarantee that nothin' 'll occur lek the foolery av last Saterday, an' that——"

"How can we guarantee such a thing?" asked Mr. Farrell.

"That's for the Committee to see to," said Terry with a sneer. "I was goin' to say also, that I must do me own work me own way an' have no grumblin' or growlin' durin' drill. Such things I—will—not—stan'!"—at each word he dug the spade-blade into the peat. "If I go out o' me way to do people gwid I expec' fair tr'atment in return."

"I thought, Terry," said Mr. Farrell, "ye looked at things in a more patriotic light than that, an' wur only doin' what any dacent man 'd do for Irelan'."

"If I *didn't* luk at things lek that," answered Terry, "ye'd not fin' Terry Fitch drillin' any granny puckins! Yis, surs, I sink me feelin's an' me pride as a trained man all because—as I hope yis very well know—I'm a thrue sort! An' wid the grace o' God I'll see things through. *But*—as I said—no interferin' av Committees; no cowardly un-sojer-lek conduc' lek we had at Rhamus; no grumblin' or growlin'—*thim's* my terms, an' they're chape."

"So they are, Terry," said Mr. Farrell, patting his shoulder, "so they are. What we'd do without you, dear only knows! But you're true owl' stock, an' the blood in ye's pure! Dang me, lads! but I cem here wid a dread on me, for Terry *has* had things to put up wid; but, thank the Lord, the dread's gone! Terry, your han' on it!"

Terry by this was considerably mollified. He even condescended to sit on the bank with the Committee and discuss matters over a pipe of tobacco. In the end these conclusions were arrived at: that the drills should continue; that Terry should act; that, for the present, the Squad should be divided into two parts, each part to meet once a week in James O'Gara's barn—the safest place, perhaps, as O'Gara was a widower—for gentle instruction; and that by word of mouth the Squad should be informed of these decisions.

Then the Committee departed, leaving Terry with a feeling of triumph at his heart.

But when Lizzie and Paddy came back, the first words he said to them were: "Ha' ye been home?"

And, receiving "No" for answer, the next words he uttered were: "Well I widn't say anything to yir mother about them gintlemin, childer. If ye do I'll switch ye!"

VII

Whilst Terry Fitch, the following Saturday night, was putting eight men—thanks to Mrs. Grogan and Terry himself, that was all of the Half-Squad that dared attend—through their facings in James O'Gara's barn, the six men from Gorteen were creeping up Rhamus Hill and taking up their positions round the castle. They placed themselves, as comfortably as was possible, at nearly equal distances in the ditch that encircles the ruins; so that each man, to his right and left, commanded a space across which no enemy might pass unobserved. Fortunately for them the night was very dark; but about nine o'clock a thick cold rain began to fall. They shivered where they lay, and, drawing their coats tightly about them, found what shelter the hedge could give them.

At nine o'clock Henry Bredin said "Whisht!" to Joseph Donaldson on his right and John Martin on his left, who, in their turn, passed on the word to the men on *their* right and left. Hardly was the word round when a man jumped the hedge between Donaldson and Bredin, and, walking swiftly to the castle, disappeared through the hole in the wall. He wore a slouched felt hat drawn over his eyes, had his coat-collar round his ears, and carried a heavy stick. More than that neither Donaldson nor Bredin could make out. Two minutes after, a second figure broke through the hedge and entered the castle. He was followed, at short intervals, by five others. Meanwhile, two men had crossed the ditch from the plantation-side between John Martin and Ned Noble, had skirted the walls, and also entered the ruins before the eyes of Donaldson and Bredin. After this, for a while no one came; then, all at once, three men—two from the road and one from the plantation—startled the watchers by mounting the ditch, whistling twice, and, being answered from the castle, breaking through the hedge almost over the heads of John Martin and Henry Bredin. These, having entered the castle, made the intruders number twelve, and caused the Six to cover their faces with their coats and lie tight. They lay like this for half-an-hour, awaiting events with doubtful hearts, their clothes by now saturated, and their limbs stiff with cold and uncomfortableness. Then, suddenly, there was a stir inside the castle, and one by one the invaders came through the walls and, with their hats well over their faces, passed out between Henry Bredin and Joseph Donaldson. The six waited for a little longer; then rose cautiously and gathered together under the sheltered wall of the castle. All looked miserable and cold and troubled. They spoke some few half-hearted words, and dolefully turned homewards.

The following Monday the whole Gorteen Squad, numbering fifty odd, assembled at their headquarters in Samuel Mires' loft. It was deemed right, the meeting being special and of grave importance, to elect a chairman; and to this honour Sergeant Mires—not because he was Samuel, you observe, but because he was Sergeant—was unanimously chosen.

Rising, the Sergeant thanked the meeting for the honour done to him; then proceeded to give his reasons for calling this general meeting of the Squad. He told how on the previous Saturday night week eighteen of their number had met to drill in Rhamus Castle, had been disturbed in the performance of their duties, and had wisely and for fear of detection fled for some distance; how he himself had to some extent investigated the cause of their alarm, but, being still in doubt, had asked the Eighteen to meet for discussion; how the Eighteen had declared their unaltered loyalty and fidelity to the cause of Freedom (cheers), had declared in favour of continuing the drills, and had resolved, prior to informing the Squad of their mishap, to try to get definite evidence to lay before a meeting; how, in pursuance of that resolve, the Eighteen had selected six of their number to collect evidence, in which mission, he thought, the Six, after much privation and at great personal risk, had to some extent succeeded—all this Sergeant Mires told at great length and with much fluency.

"Ye now know all I wish to tell ye," said the Sergeant in conclusion; "and I now call upon Henry Marvin to give an account of his adventure last Saturday night on Rhamus Hill."

As the Sergeant sat down, certain young men at the back of the meeting set up a commotion, calling to one another, going from one to another, and indulging in noisy laughter, till the Sergeant was obliged to hammer his table violently and call "Silence!" in big tones.

Presently the disorder ceased, and Henry Marvin rose. He said:—"Last Saterday we—that is to say, Joe Donaldson, John Martin, Henry Bredin, Dick Hoey, Ned Noble, an' meself—set out after dark for Rhamus Castle. Arrived there, we conc'aled ourselves in the ditch roun' the castle, an', in spite av the rain an' the cowld, waited there about an hour an' a half. 'Twas long afore any wan cem; but, at last, a man passed between Donaldson an' Bredin an' went in. He wus foll'ed by others, till, what wid what passed meself an' what cem from other parts, twenty or thirty men in all had assembled. They wur all ruffianly-lukin' blaggards, wid slouched hats an' big sticks, an' wur all big an' hard-lukin'. Wid the blackness av the night an' their style av dress, we couldn't see who they wur; but, from all appearance, they wur Fenians av the blackest dye."

Here some one laughed outright, and several young men were seen to smother their emotion in red pocket-handkerchiefs. Sergeant Mires again demanded silence, and Henry went on.

"I don't know what yis have to laugh at down there," he said, caustically; "if it's at yir own ignerance an' foolery, yi're well employed; but if it's at what I'm sayin', yi'd be better outside wid the pigs. I see who's laughin', an' I advise them to keep quiet. As I was sayin', afore this interruption, these twenty or thirty blaggards took possession av the castle. I wus minded to pass roun' the word to stale up to the walls an' have a peep, but wus afeerd we mightn't be able to see in the dark; an' there's an ould sayin' that discretion 's the best part o' valour. So we lay on in the cowld an' rain for about an hour, an' then the whole band o' blaggards cem out an' disappeared down the hill. We wur too stiff an' wet for pursuit; so, after comparin' notes, we cem home. If me opinion is axed as to what the whole thing meant, I say— an' I say it only after a dale o' thought—this Squad was meant to be massacreed last Saterday night in cowld blood be a parcel o' blood-thirsty rebels. Fortunately, we didn't give them the chance; if we had, yon rascals, armed as they wur to the teeth, 'd ha' killed uz where we stud."

Henry's speech made a great sensation. Men held up their hands in righteous horror, and swelled with holy indignation. For a while the meeting gave reins to its voice and imagination; and it was not till Sergeant Mires had raised his voice to a shout, and had banged his fist sore on the table, that he succeeded in quelling the tumult. Then he called upon Ned Noble to corroborate Henry Marvin's statement.

Ned's speech was, as may be imagined, neither modest nor nervous. The big drum in the corner could not have equalled its windy volume of sound and clatter. Ned himself seemed to be blown with patriotic fervour; nor did he fail to make his evidence worthy of the man and the occasion. The twelve, that had swelled to twenty or thirty with Henry Marvin, became forty or fifty with Ned. Their appearance he described as "shockin' to behold," "lek a tribe o' divils from hell," "the scum o' the earth armed to the teeth." He said he "trimbled where he stud to think o' the shockin' massacree that was intended;" he declared how thankful to Providence he was to have escaped unhurt from such dangers. Said he: "I'm no man to boast much, but I think I may luk back on our work wid pride. We did little, it's true, but we seen a power. We seen enough, men, to make the bouldest shake in their shoes. We seen——What the divil are ye laughin' at down there, Johnny Jago? I've been watchin' ye for some time—you an' John Joe Neil—yir conduc' is disgraceful. How can wan spake, Sergeant Mires, wid such carryin' on? I propose all these young shavers be turned out!"

"Hear, hear!" went up the shout; and the Chairman, rising, called on Johnny Jago for an explanation of his unseemly conduct. Johnny was unwilling to rise. Voices urged him to "stand up and tell all," to "spake out," to "show things in their true light."

After five minutes of noise and entreaty, and table hammering and strong talk from the Chair, Johnny slowly got to his feet;

but, seeing the crowd of faces turned towards him, lost courage, and sat down with a rush. Again he was urged to rise, and again he essayed to speak. This time he managed to say that the cause of his laughter was Ned Noble's remark that he was not a man to boast. As he sat down his companions called his names and turned from him with disgust. But Ned Noble jumped up and said he was much obliged to young Jago, but he would like to know what made him laugh *before* he (Ned) made the remark referred to? Thereupon the voices rose once more: "Spit it out, Johnny!" "Come, Johnny, be a man!" "Ye've nothin' to fear, Johnny; spake up!"

It was now plain to the meeting at large that some secret lurked in its midst; so with one voice it demanded Johnny Jago to explain. But Johnny would not. No; divil a foot; he wouldn't be bullied by any man or men. The meeting rose and roared. "Roar away," called Jago. Then Dick Foster jumped to his feet, spread out his hand, and called for a hearing. But the meeting wanted Jago, and Jago it would have.

"I'll spake for Jago!" shouted Dick.

"No, no; we want Jago," cried the meeting.

"I'll tell ye what Jago meant to say," shouted Dick; "I know all."

And the hubbub ceased.

"What I've got to say," said Dick—he was a self-confident young fellow, with a good presence and a loud voice—" 'll be short an' sweet, lek an ass's gallop. If Johnny Jago's laughed much this blessed night he's had gwid r'ason to, an' so has more than him. Some av uz this end o' the loft have had plenty to do to keep from brustin'. For meself the sweat's dreepin' down me back wid tryin' to keep a straight face. Mebbe some o' ye 'll laugh too when ye hear the joke: mebbe some o' ye won't; but as ye will have it, here y' are. When some av uz got word the tail-end av last week that there'd be no drill, we wondered, av coorse. An' in the coorse av some chat we had together we swapped notions, an' havin' nothin' better to do, set ourselves to fin' a cause. So one av uz went here an' one there axin' different members o' the Squad if they knew the cause. Then we met again, an' divil a one av uz knew a hate 'cep' one man; an' who he heerd from is nather here nor there. He didn't know much, ather, but what he did know was enough to make uz see how things stud. An' we, bein' young frisky chaps, put our heads together an' drew out a plan for a spree. On the Saterday night we took big sticks, an' disguisin' ourselves as well as we cud, set out for Rhamus; intendin' if we foun' foes to make them jump, an' not expectin' to fin' frien's at all, it bein' understood there'd be no drill. We waited there a while, mebbe half-an-hour, an' seein' no one, an' not carin' for the weather, we cem home jist as wise, an' about half as frisky, as when we started. That's the whole story; an' I think, from the faces I see aroun' me, it explains a power, an' excuses such av uz as wur foolish enough to laugh."

Now, the men of Gorteen are heavy a little in their wits. They can see as far as anyone through a stone wall, but they must not be hurried in the process. It was some time, therefore, before the majority of the meeting seized on the kernel of the situation. At first they were impatient with Dick; next, seeing he had somewhat to say, interested; then, as he told who the murdering villains really were, they drew in their breath with a hiss and looked at each other; then they were indignant with the Eighteen, with Sergeant Mires for his bleather, with Henry Marvin and Ned Noble for their windy nonsense.—The majority singled out Henry and Ned and looked slyly at them.

Why, the Six had been fooled; had sat in the rain in fear and trembling of their friends; had made up a story and come there and had been found out, exposed, made ridiculous! Oh, there was the joke! Ha, ha! Gorteen saw it at last! Ha, ha! It was the Six! Look at them sitting there shamefaced and angry! Oh, dear! oh, dear! Lord, did ever you hear anything better! Listen to the laughing! Look at the Six themselves—why, they're laughing too! Ay, ay! all but Henry Marvin. What the divil's he up to now? Whisht there till we hear him! Whisht! Whisht!

"I want to ax Mr. Foster a question or two," said Henry, rising calmly and speaking with cold deliberation. "First av all, I'd lek to know who gev him his infermation?"

"To that," said Dick, "I answer at once: ye won't know."

"Is that the answer of all o' ye?" asked Henry.

"It is," said the offenders.

"Ah," said Henry, "now I know who most o' the men are. Thank ye; that's one point. I can fin' out th' other for meself. Now I'd lek to know, Mr. Foster, if any of you knew that we—the six of us—'d be at Rhamus last Saterday night?"

"G' luck!" answered Dick; "ye won't catch me again. I'll answer no more."

"Very well, then," said Henry, "I take yir answer to mane Yes. Who towld ye that, now?"

"Yi're a liar!" shouted Dick; "no one knew anything about ye. I wish we had, an' we'd 'a' made it hot for ye."

"Thank ye again," said Henry; "the wish is as good as the deed, as the sayin' is. Keep on answerin', young man. Nex', wid ye tell me how many av yis wur there—the exact number?"

No answer came to this.

"Very well, then," said Henry, mounting a chair, "I'll count ye."

He counted as far as thirty-nine, when Dick Foster rose in a rage and shouted: "Yi're a liar again! there wus only twelve av uz."

Henry got down from his chair with much deliberation.

"That's good," said he. "Now I know all I want to know. Gentlemen," he said to the meeting, "I ax ye to publicly expel these members for disobeyin' orders in goin' to Rhamus Castle last Saterday."

Thereupon ensued a stormy and warm discussion. Now that the laughter was all over, some of the senior members of the Squad began to see that the exploit of the young men might have resulted in very serious consequences, and might have been the cause of publishing the doings of the Squad to the world. Besides that, the young men themselves had been guilty of very frivolous and disrespectful conduct that night; and one of their number had used very strong language towards a worthy and senior member of the Squad. Against these serious ones were arrayed all the younger members, and those who thought a joke a joke, and young men young men, and themselves thankful for a good roaring laugh.

The debate lasted an hour—and such an hour of invective, brilliant attack, hot defence, sarcasm, high words, and intense excitement never before passed in Gorteen—and was stopped only by the earnest pleading for decency and order of Sergeant Mires. He asked that the whole subject be dropped and forgotten. But Henry Marvin's side would not hear of such timorous shuffling. They demanded that a vote of the meeting be taken, and that the meeting abide by and act on the result of that vote. This furnished material for another stormy debate; and it was not till far in the night that at last nature asserted itself, and the sweating, parched, exhausted meeting agreed to come to and abide by a show of hands.

For the proposal that the Twelve be expelled the Squad, twenty-nine hands were shown; against the proposal, Sergeant Mires could count only twenty-six.

The Twelve, therefore, were to be expelled.

Henry Marvin called on Sergeant Mires to do his duty. The sergeant refused.

"Then I'll do it," said Henry, mounting his chair.

But the Twelve had heard quite enough of Henry. They rose in a body and, followed by their sympathisers, left the meeting.

Thus the Gorteen Squad reduced itself to twenty-nine; and, as Sergeant Mires was not one of them, and the late misadventure at Rhamus was still a mystery, these twenty-nine determined, before they parted, to postpone further drilling for a period.

VIII

The split in the Gorteen Squad naturally was productive of much ill-blood and evil speaking in that very respectable townland. It is even declared that more than one bloody combat took place because of it; and that Henry Marvin for some time went about in great fear of personal violence. Time, however, to some extent healed the breach, and soon their crops and turf gave the men of Gorteen other things to think about.

Meanwhile, in Bilboa things had not been going satisfactorily. Terry Fitch, if more gentle, had yet been sufficiently tactless and truculent to account for the absence of more than one of the Twenty-five from drill. Mr. Dooley had found other and more congenial employment for his great intellect in the preliminaries of what promised to be a famous General Election. Mr. Farrell, it is true, had stood to his guns and relaxed none of his vigour and enthusiasm, but he had met with annoying and unexpected troubles. At first the Squad had turned out with some regularity and punctuality. Then gradually a falling off in the attendance had shown itself. A man would come one night and not come the next, or would come twice and not again for perhaps three drills, or would leave early one night and come late the next, or would promise faithfully to come and yet not come. All this had been irritating to Mr. Farrell. Of course he had done his utmost to make men come; but for all his banter, and earnest appeals, and personal threats, he had received only half-hearted excuses, and sly looks, and lying promises. Do what he would the men had failed to come regularly and to take that patriotic interest in the drills which he expected. Of the Twenty-five, James O'Gara alone had been ever faithful, and he was a widower. Could evidence be plainer? Biddy Grogan had done her work well—and woman's tongue, and tricks, and insidious influence had beaten patriotism and Mr. Farrell from the field. Then came the fine weather, with all its weary toils, and with it the Bilboa men, like the men of Gorteen, disbanded themselves for a period.

That summer the country was agitated by the strife of parties. A General Election was held, and concerning it may be written two things: Mr. Dooley became Member of Parliament for his native county; and the hand of the law was relaxed over Ireland in consequence of a change of Government. Both these results were received with joy in Bilboa; and when the harvest was nearly over, Mr. Farrell went to the houses of the Twenty-five, and to many more in the neighbourhood, and spoke with such freedom and point, that the eyes of the women were opened, and the patriotic enthusiasm of the men rekindled with tenfold ardour. There was no longer any need for very great secrecy, Mr. Farrell showed, and people were freer to do and say what they liked. Provided they behaved soberly and minded their own business, there was no need for fear. "Men, men!" said Mr. Farrell, "work for yourselves if ye won't for your country. Now's the day and now's the hour! There's glory awaitin' us, if we only be wise. An' the wife who hinders any man in the pursuit av his duty's a traitor—woman as she is."

So the Bilboa Squad, greatly augmented and this time firmly established, was once more called to parade and answered with skirls of enthusiasm. Terry Fitch was again instructor; Mr. Farrell was now President as well as Secretary; but of the movements of Mr. Dooley one must not write.

Nor were the Gorteen boys idle. They also were called to parade; and at a monster meeting that reeked of whisky, came to each others arms and reorganised the Squad. Then also it was resolved that a deputation should wait upon Lord Lowth with a view to the re-establishment of The Lowth Castle Infantry, whose motto was "Croppies, Lie Down."

So one day six of the Squad, among whom were our old friends Henry Marvin and Samuel Mires, crossed Lough Erne at Garvagh, and took the road for Lowth Castle. Arrived there, a servant took them along a terrace and left them standing by an open window.

Presently a voice came from inside.

"Well?" said the voice.

"We've come, me Lord," said Samuel Mires, "on important an' private business."

"What is it all about?"

"It relates, me Lord," said Henry Marvin, "to a resolution passed at a meeting of yir loyal an' faithful tenantry."

"And who are you?" asked the voice.

"We're a deputation, me Lord," answered Henry, "impowered to carry you that resolution."

"Well, what is it?"

"We've got it in writin', me Lord," answered Samuel Mires, "an' we'd rather yi'd read it."

THE AWKWARD SQUADS

A servant came to the window, and from the bare-headed deputation received the resolution on a silver salver.

Presently the voice was heard reading the resolution in measured tones; then: "Well, you'd better come in here."

Whilst the deputation were wondering how this was to be achieved, the footman came again to the window and directed them to go round to the big back door. There a second footman took them in charge, and loftily conducted them through many passages till they came to Lord Lowth's room. Here the first footman received and ushered them into the august presence of their noble landlord.

He sat—a small, middle-aged aristocrat—behind a littered table in the corner of a great room. He gave the deputation five minutes in which to admire the paintings on the wall and the splendours of the fittings, whilst he finished the writing of a letter. Then he leaned back in his chair and surveyed the deputation from top to toe.

"Well?" said he presently.

Samuel Mires stepped forward, and, nervously fumbling with the brim of his hat, asked if his Lordship had been graciously pleased to peruse the resolution.

"Yes," said his Lordship.

"Then may it please yir Lordship," said Samuel, "what does yir Lordship think of it?"

"What is it all about?" asked my Lord.

Samuel and Henry in turn, and sometimes both together, gave the history and purport of the resolution.

"H'm!" said his Lordship, and gave himself for a moment to deep thought. Then: "It's all very well for you fellows to ask me to give you something to amuse yourselves. You forget the expense to me and the hostile criticism that is sure to follow the reorganisation of my Yeomanry Corps. Besides, what are the duties of yeomen? To protect the life and property of the landlord! And you want me to re-form the Corps, so that you may protect your own lives!"

Henry Marvin humbly demurred. He said that the first wish of their heart was to protect his Lordship from enemies, his noble mansion, and his gracious family; that their second wish was to guard their principles and their religion; and their third to protect themselves, that they might long occupy and cultivate his Lordship's property.

"If I start this Corps again," answered his Lordship, "will you guarantee that I bear no expense in the matter of—of uniform or arms, and all that?"

Samuel Mires replied that all the old uniforms and arms were still available; and that all his Lordship was humbly asked to do was to give the movement his sanction, and in his condescension occasionally to review the Corps.

"And it must be understood that for any violences against law and order, and any breaches of the peace by the Corps, I shall not be answerable or be liable to be called to account."

Most assuredly his Lordship might rest satisfied on that head.

"And the Corps will, I suppose, maintain itself at a proper state of efficiency, and try to reach its old high standard of loyalty and decency?"

"The same men, yir Lordship," answered Henry Marvin, "who formerly were proud to defend you from harm, will now swear to defend you an' themselves an' their religion an' country from foes an' rebels."

"Then," said his Lordship, "I agree to your proposal, provided that I am not passing the bounds of the law and that I don't see fit cause to change my mind. You will, of course, furnish me with full particulars of your movements and trouble me as little as possible. I hope all of you are working hard at your farms and getting your rents together. It is a proud boast of mine that I am one of the few landowners in this unfortunate country who still tries to uphold the old amicable relations between landlord and tenant—and—and is rewarded—rewarded in some sort—by punctuality and gratitude in the payment of his rents. Good-day to you."

His Lordship rang a bell, and gave a footman directions to take "these men" to the butler for some refreshment; upon which the deputation, with profound thanks to his Lordship for his condescension, withdrew to the servants' hall, where they were plentifully helped to bread and cheese and ale by the hall-boy, and, finally, sent on their way rejoicing through the back door.

So the Lowth Castle Infantry once more paraded in gaudy array, under the command of Samuel Mires, now a full-blown Sergeant-major, and swelled their chests in their red tunics as their legs swung to the inspiriting strains of six fifes and a big drum belaboured by big Ned Noble.

The occasion was their first church parade. From far and near people flocked to see them; clustered along the roadway, climbed the walls and gate-posts of the churchyard, crowded the tombstones, and gave the Rev. Mr. Black the finest congregation that had ever filled the high-backed and straight-backed pews of Drumhill Church. In the front pews facing the pulpit were the Infantry in pipe-clay and scarlet; to the right was Lord Lowth, in all the pride of ownership and pedigree; to the left sat the neighbouring gentry; and away down the aisles, up in the three galleries, stretching through the open door into the graveyard, was the great host of rustic manhood and beauty and youth. And as the girls picked out their sweethearts among the Infantry, and the men, under the influence of Mr. Black's stirring words, felt their hearts swell at the memory of stirring deeds of old, curious lads were wondering why some of the red tunics were disfigured with little square patches, beneath which were dark, strange stains—stains that made those who knew shudder.

Once again that year the Yeomen turned out in full force, and, in all the pride and majesty of military array, marched to the ferry, crossed the lake, and, with Sergeant-major Mires before the drum and fifes, swung along to Lowth Castle, where they were reviewed by their Commander and publicly commended for their appearance and smartness.

The review over, a shooting contest began for prizes and, what was of more value, a whole year's glory for those fortunate enough to win them. One must say fortunate, for the old smooth-bore carabines that were used carried the bullets to the mark more by good luck than good guidance. Indeed, the winner of the third prize made a proud boast of the fact that the solitary outer which formed his score was achieved with his eyes shut. There were two bulls'-eyes made that day, and the target was the luckiest object within range of the Corps. Not that the shooting was bad—few there would have missed a flying wild duck—but the guns were wonderful in their inaccuracy. Once during the contest a thing happened which might have been tragic in its results. Someone put two charges of powder behind one of Ned Noble's bullets. He bore the shock manfully; but he wrathfully declared that the rascal who played the trick would, if Ned could find him—and he had his suspicions—pay the penalty at the sharp end of Ned's bayonet. Most fortunately, the culprit was not found; for Ned was powerful in his moments of anger.

Powder wasted and glory achieved, the Yeomen sat down to dinner in a huge marquee, and played havoc with the cold beef and mustard and bread and cheese. More reputations were made at the feast than at the butts. To this day it is told in Gorteen, how Ned Noble drowned his wrath in seventeen horns of ale without so much as turning a hair; and how Henry Marvin emptied six in succession without taking his hand from the muzzle of his Queen Bess. Then also was uttered the saying—now almost a proverb in Gorteen—of Richard Hoey, who, with his mouth crammed with bread and meat, declared that he, being toothless, preferred champ (mashed potatoes) to any kind of flesh-meat. Nor is it forgotten how fluently and cleverly Sergeant-major Mires proposed the health of Lord Lowth, how enthusiastically the Corps honoured the toast, and how humorously and unaffectedly Lord Lowth replied.

But at last the day ended; and, with well-filled belts, the Yeomen shouldered their arms and marched for home.

What followed is historic. Passing through the half-darkness of Kilpad Wood, the Corps was set upon by a swarm of men armed with heavy sticks. It is said that the attackers outnumbered the attacked by two to one; but rumour is wrong: both sides were as nearly as possible equal in point of numbers.

At first the Gorteen boys in their flurry and surprise gave way somewhat; but, presently, recovering their breath and their self-possession, they rallied manfully, and, fighting shoulder to shoulder, were soon on terms with their foes. To their credit be it said that they scorned to use their side-arms, and faced the whizzing blackthorns with gun-butts and belt-buckles. They fought well, with stubborn fury and watchful fierceness, against opponents who were agile as cats and excited as furies. On the one side the cry was "King William for ever!" On the other, "*Erin go bragh!*" The Squads had met at last!

Up and down the road the fight waged fiercely, noisily, unmercifully. Off came the tunics and the frieze-coats to give freer elbow play. Crack went the sticks and thud went the gun-butts. Up went Bilboa's skirls and yells, answered by the hoarse angry shouts of Gorteen. Up and down the road the fight waged, among the trees, swelled out to the open fields—till heads were broken and shoulders sore, and the ground was littered with men lying among red coats and shakos, frieze coats and blackthorns, and those who still fought on were weary and breathless.

Big Ned was down with Henry Marvin and Sergeant Mires; all the veterans were lying groaning; only the younger men—Jago, Dick Foster, and the rest—were left to face Terry the Tough, still performing valiantly before a hardy little band.

"Come on! Come on, ye divils!" cried Terry. "Irelan' for ever—an' to blazes wi' King Billy!"

"Down wi' the croppies!" shouted back the remnant of Gorteen; "an' to hell wi' the Pope!"

So up and down the road, among the trees, out into the open fields the battle raged—till even these had had enough, and darkness fell and parted what were left of the rival Squads.

It was a glorious fight, worthy of the tradition of old Ireland, manfully fought, stubbornly endured—a fight which abundantly proved that Irishmen are still able to settle their little difficulties, whether social or political, by force of their own right arms.

May the Awkward Squads never meet in a worse cause!

A STATE OFFICIAL

Right in the heart of Cavan, sheltered on all sides by hills, and scattered aimlessly along two roads which there meet, cross, and wander on, stands the village of Raheen. In a generous moment you might say it numbered twenty houses, all thickly whitewashed, heavily thatched, and preserving a stillness that might be taken as peaceful or dull as the humour required.

Coming down the hill on which, amid its mouldering graves, stands the parish church, and over which lies the road to the railway, you see right in front, under an arch of spreading beech branches, the village shop cleverly placed on an angle made by the crossing roads; and to the left a low grey wall over which peep the white chimneys of a row of thatched cottages. These last really make the village: without them (and the shop maybe) two roads would meet at a hamlet after their wanderings across the hills.

But, besides this mere numerical and purely local importance, the cottages still preserve a certain air of distinction, first assumed when a tyrannical, to be sure, yet, on the whole, intelligent, Government decided that they should shelter a branch of the Imperial post-office. It is gone now; but some time, say ten years ago, if, one evening in June, you had leant over the low grey wall and looked down, you would have seen, across a trim, gay little garden and behind a wealth of hanging creepers, an open window framing the bent head of old Dan the cobbler and village postmaster. The *tip tap* of his hammer would have come with a soothing regularity and seemed to be the only sign of life—at that hour it would certainly be the only sound—in the place. After the dust of the road you would have found it pleasant to lean there on the cool stones, and, with that dull beating in your ears, let your eyes wander idly over the homely garden, the old brown thatch, then across the roof towards the fading green of the hills.

But presently the sound would cease; then, looking, you would have seen Dan lean forward, turn a leaf in a book that lay on the window-ledge before him, read fixedly for a moment, and, with a smile on his old face, look up at yourself. For your elbows would rest on stones that were shiny from long rubbing by the coats of gossips who had stood there, sometimes by the hour, cracking a sly joke with the garrulous old man.

Had you remained longer that evening, however, you would have seen a thin, ugly man turn down by the end of the wall, cross the garden, and, regardless of tender flowers, tramp clumsily to Dan's window.

"Hello!" said Dan, looking up and pushing his spectacles up his brow; "that's sudden. Ah, it's you, Micky! Well, God be with ye, me son, anyway; but you're a powerful bad friend to the light."

"Yis," said the man, "I suppose I am—but no matter. I want to say a word to ye."

"Say on, me son," said Dan, reaching to close his book, and putting down his hammer. "As the wise man said, 'There's a time for all things.'"

"I want to know, Dan," said the other, stooping and resting his hands on the windowsill, "if you've thought better o' what ye said th' other night? Ha' ye changed yir mind?"

"Eh, avick? What's that?" said Dan sharply. "Changed me mind?—that's what I seldom do. What about?"

"Ye know."

"I forget then."

"About the man that's occupyin' Widow Reilly's farm—are ye goin' to do lek another?"

"Ah!" said Ned, "that's it, is it? An' why should I do lek another? Eh?"

"It's no use bleatherin'!" answered the man irritably. "Ye know what I mane—In plain words will ye quit spakin' or havin' anythin' to do wi' the man?"

"Why should I, Micky? Answer me that. Why *should* I luk your way for advice?"

"It's not me. I do as I'm bid—so must you. The man's betrayed the cause be takin' an evicted woman's farm—ye know that. So long as he's there he's a traitor to the cause, an' them that has dealin's with him are worse."

"The *cause!*" broke in Dan with a scornful laugh. "Ye call it a cause to leave a man without a bite to eat, or a dud to wear, or a soul to cross words with! D'ye call it a cause to let wee childer starve an' a woman to fret?"

"Ye may quit!" said the man abruptly. "Say no more; ivery word takes ye deeper. Is that your answer?"

"Micky Flynn," said Dan, rising and, the better to look severe, dragging his spectacles down to his nose, "from you or any other man I take no counsel when I try to do right. Ye call it a *cause*. I say it's hellish persecution! The man has harmed no one, neither have his childer; he's only done what *you* think wrong. An' who are you, Micky Flynn, to judge another? *I* think he's done no harm, Micky; an' cause or no cause I'm goin' to think lek that." He stooped and laid his hand on the closed book. "Here's where I get me counsel, Micky—here I read"—he shook a warning finger at the man—"*'This above all—to thine own self be true, and it must——'*"

The man turned away with a foul exclamation of disgust and spat on the flowers, walked to the gate, and there wheeled round.

"Ye may talk yir fool's clack to yirself, now," he shouted back. "Be God yi 'll have time enough! ye bleatherin' ould rogue!"

Dan leaned across the sill and looked at his flowers.

"Ah!" said he, "it's well there's rain comin'; it 'll help to wipe out the divil's hoof-tracks." Then he laughed, and closing the window lit a candle and sat down on his stool.

The unsteady light fell softly on all the mad disorder of the room—the litter on the floor, the rolls of leather in the corner, the lasts on the wall hanging over pictured newspaper cuttings, the little official desk strewn with old pens, cheap stationery, dirty copies of rules and regulations—fell softly on all that and on the sturdy old figure of the postmaster. He laughed softly to himself, and wagged his head gravely.

"Well, well," said he, "after all these years o' peace an' quiet to come to this! Spoke to lek that! What next? What's goin' to come to me? Well, well; time 'll tell. *'This above all,'*" he muttered slowly, "*'to thine own self be true—to thine own self be true.'*"

He reached for his book, and, holding the candle close to his face, began turning the leaves and reading a line here and there on a chance page.

"*'My way of life is fallen into the sere, the yellow leaf'*—ah, ah!

"*'Rude am I in my speech.'* Just so, just so!

"'*I am a very foolish, fond old man . . . climbing sorrow . . . serpent's tooth.*' Poor old Lear, Lord help all like him!"

Presently he looked up, and, pushing back his glasses, declaimed in a measured sing-song:

"'*There's a divinity that shapes our ends, rough-hew them how we will.*' That's good! that's what I wanted—that's somethin' to sleep on—that an' th' other. What's this it is? Oh, ay! '*This above all . . . There's a divinity.*'"

Repeating the phrases over and over to himself, he rose and busied himself about the room, arranging his tools, tidying his desk, looking out his work for the morrow.

"'*There's a divinity,*'" he kept on repeating; then suddenly stopped, and holding up a piece of wax-end, "'Shapes our *ends!*'" he said with a soft chuckle. "I wonder if it takes a divinity to shape this?"

And laughing at his little joke he bolted the door and went to bed.

The next morning, his flowers watered and wed, his frugal breakfast over, and his little kitchen swept and tidied, Dan with his book open before him, and breathing the sweet morning freshness of his garden, was again at his work, hammering and sewing, reading and muttering, laughing softly betimes to himself and looking up through his spectacles at the wall. But though he looked up often no one that morning leant on the stones to exchange greetings or jokes; sometimes footsteps sounded from the road; sometimes a neighbour passed close to the wall; once or twice someone looked furtively towards the open window: but no one spoke; and for the first time for many years the stool at Dan's elbow, where usually his neighbours waited for the post, was vacant.

"Eh?" he would say, looking round at the empty stool and up at the wall. "Eh? well, well!"

Then the post came, carried by a lad who that morning seemed peculiarly gruff and silent, and Dan, for a while sinking his trade and putting on the air of importance becoming a state official, carefully sorted the letters and placed them in order on his desk.

"Now," said he, turning to his work again, "*now* they'll come—they *must* come now; they *must*."

Only children came that morning—children who seemed suddenly to be smitten with an unusual awkwardness and shyness, as they stopped before the window or came to the door of Dan's room and asked if there were any letters for Mammy, please.

"Come in, Mary, agra!" Dan called cheerily to the first who came; "come in, me girl, an' I'll give ye a flower.—Ye can't come?—Well, well!—Where's your Daddy the day?—Eh? Where's your tongue, Mary?"

The child suddenly raised her hand from her lips to her eyes, and began to cry.

"Oh!" she sobbed, "please Dan, Mammy says I musn't spake to ye."

Dan's eyes swiftly became grave behind his spectacles.

"Ah!" he said. "Well, well!"—then, without a word, handed the child the letter.

With the next it was the same, and the next—after that he questioned no more. And all that day he sat silent, his book for the most part neglected, and his heart heavy; not one came to his little room, not one paused to speak to him, not one looked over the wall, except towards evening, when Dan, more by habit than will, raising his eyes, saw a dark, ugly face, that scowled on him for a moment and was gone.

So three days passed; and the fourth morning saw Dan cobbler no longer, but post-master only. The last job of mending had been taken away (by a child, as usual); for the first time in his working life he had not a stitch to sew. For three days he had been left to his thoughts and his book—in that time only once had he heard a friendly voice, and that belonged to the man for whom he was suffering. His heart was heavy; his flowers had not their old sweet power over him; even Shakespeare could not wholly catch his thoughts; his eyes were grown very sorrowful, and his brow was troubled.

"Well, well!" he would say, "well, well!—Am I asleep or awake? Is it me at all?—What have I done?—What am I to do?"

For the hundredth time he reviewed his position. He was cut off from the world—a social outlaw. He had no work, would have none. He could only get food by walking far to a town where he was not known. He had the few shillings a week that made his official salary, and a few pounds in the savings bank—could he keep life with that? He had that one friend—a dull fellow, as it happened, without a laugh in his body, whom, besides, it was dangerous just then to visit. His own thoughts, himself, bare life, his little cottage and garden—could he do with just that?

Such was his position, and such it would be for long and long—till he yielded. Was it worth while? he asked. Should he yield? He did no one any good by holding out—not one, not even that dull friend. He was pleasing himself, injuring himself. Should he yield? he asked himself that fourth morning, sitting on his stool beside his open window waiting for the children to come for the letters. Mechanically his hand reached for his book of wisdom and opened its old, tattered pages.

"'*This above all,*'" he said in a little while, raising his beaming face to the wall. "'*This above all, to thine own self be true*'—an' what's th' other? '*There's a divinity that shapes our ends.*'—Just so,

Dan; that's your reason. By the Lord, Dan, you're a sinner at heart; only for the old book you'd be a limb of Satan!"

So he accepted his position; and for a time bore his lot cheerfully, passing the long days as best he might—working in his garden, whitewashing his cottage inside and out and repairing its thatch, reading his one book by the open window; sometimes, at night, dressing in his Sunday clothes, and, with his hat jauntily cocked and a flower in his coat, whistling and singing defiantly as he slowly paraded up and down the street or past his neighbours' open doors.

For a time—say, a few weeks longer—he bore himself bravely; then, with a sudden rush, was borne in upon him a full sense of his cruel, unutterable loneliness. A living man shut in a tomb; a tongue quickly smitten dumb; a world suddenly changed from life and laughter to grim, gloomy silence: as such, in such, he found himself. Could he endure that—he by nature so sociable and kindly, who, lately, had been the life of the village—its half-understood (crazy, indeed, people said) wit, sage, politician; he who had delighted in the talk and society of his neighbours as much as in his own musings? Could he endure silence, loneliness, not for a day or a week, but for long, perhaps very long? He was doing right; but that did not bring comfort enough—indeed was but cold comfort, seeing that doing right brought only trouble. He could bear hunger, privation, neglect; but silence, loneliness, this death in life, these he could not bear. He felt he must talk or go mad. And all round him for miles and miles there was not one with whom he could chat pleasantly for an hour in the day, only an hour; not one but the dull, distant fellow for whom he was denying himself.

Yes, there was another; he, at least, would listen patiently.

So Dan took his book, and, climbing the hill behind the shop, came at last to a hovel by the wayside, where, bending over a small peat-fire, he found a miserable old man, clad in rags, crippled with age, dirty beyond belief, and with only bare life lighting his eyes. Here was someone who would listen, even if he could not answer; a relic almost of life, mumbling childishly about himself and his pains, sometimes knitting his brows as his tongue fashioned an old-time phrase, or his mind was troubled with a sudden, half-realised memory.

"Ah!" he would mutter, "it's shivery cowld the day—Tell me, did—did—was it true that they disestablished the Church, the Prodestan'—? —ach, no!—ach, a bad man!"

And so he muttered now and then, whilst Dan read by the hour, or stopped to expound a passage, or, coming at last to his favourite lines, made them the text of a long harangue in which his tongue freed his mind of the irritating, ugly burden gathered through those days of silence.

"Ach, a bad man!" was the response, or one equally vague. "Ach, a bad man!"

But for all his squalor and witlessness, the old cripple was a human being who listened to Dan and did not keep his face from him; who turned his head and said "Good morning" when Dan entered, and followed him with lifeless old eyes as he went—a human being to whom Dan could talk, and who answered as best he could.

This was very well, so far: but, returning one day from one of these morning visits; feeling, for all his recent effort, a great desire to talk (really, it may be, a craving for fellowship and sympathy), an almost irresistible impulse to shout aloud, or to go to the nearest house and there compel conversation, and wondering betimes how best he should put behind him the long remaining hours of the day; suddenly, right in view of the village, the thought came to him—Why not go and talk? Who might hinder him? People might not answer; but they could not refuse to hear.

The notion made him laugh and slap his leg as he stood pondering on the road. It would be a good way to pay back men's cruelty; it would give himself pleasure and them annoyance; perhaps—yes, perhaps!—he might be able to mingle wisdom with his talk, and so gradually bring them round to his charitable point of view.

"Yes," he said aloud, slapping his leg once more, and beaming at the thought of the funny, clever, old codger he still was; "yes, begob, it's a good idea—a good idea, me son! Dan, you're not done with yet! I'll try it this very night—Mebbe, mebbe—" And, turning over the may-bes in his mind, he went slowly, but not sadly, home.

That evening, with his book under his arm, and a big rose in his black chapel coat, Dan went out; and, taking his stand about the crossing of the roads, before the shop and within hearing of the cottages, there, with a humorous glint in his eye which sometimes belied the seriousness of his face, read, expounded, and discoursed.

Had you been in Raheen that fine summer's evening; enjoying the rich warmth of the sunset, perhaps, as you leaned at the old spot across the wall; you must certainly have watched the scene with interest—the laughing, bare-armed women at the doors; the men lounging against the wall, wondering whether Dan were knave or fool; the children in the dusty, yellow street clustering, open-eyed, round the old man just then raising his voice in a part serious, part humorous discourse on Truth even in politics to one's self, and the Divinity that even in politics shapes man's ends. You would have found the scene interesting; perhaps, had you known what lay behind it all, you might have found it pathetic.

Only, the villagers clearly found in it nothing but amusement and a little welcome excitement; for, a night or two after saw

Dan talking to bare white walls, the doors all closed, the children's voices coming merrily over the roofs from the back. But Dan was not discomfited. He moved closer to the cottages, and raised his voice louder in a more personal and less humorous harangue—yes! waxed bold; and one night, entering a house, stood with his back to the door and spoke his soul concerning the cause and its adherents.

This, in the opinion of his neighbours, was more than amusing and not to be tolerated. He might talk nonsense outside as much as he chose; but a man's hearthstone was private, and the cause was sacred. He might be cracked—no doubt he was; but he had sense enough left to do harm and talk black heresy.

He had one more chance; and, recklessly, almost foolishly abused it. Then a party of men, with blackened faces and carrying guns, visited him as he sat in his kitchen reading by candle light. They entered silently; and, having surrounded him with a ring of threatening muzzles, one of their number, in forcible language, made clear to the trembling, haggard old man the character and blackness of his offence and the swift punishment that would follow its repetition.

Did he hear? shouted the man, and fired at the roof.

Then, silently they went out, and left the old man to stagger to bed with a great pain at his heart.

The next morning another opened the post-bag; and now, people say that sometimes at night, if you lean over the wall, across the rotting flower-beds you will see a laughing, muttering old man behind a closed window, hammering and reading away.

THEY THAT MOURN

Bunn Market was over its hurry and haggle. In corners and quiet spots of the big market-yard you saw men and women carefully counting their little stores of silver, testing the coins with their teeth, knotting them firmly in red pocket-handkerchiefs, finally stowing them away in their long, wide pockets as cautiously as though every sixpence were a diamond. In the streets, people were leisurely moving towards the shops, where tills were rattling and counters teeming, and trade, for a few hours, mightily flourishing, after its whole six days of blissful stagnation.

A cart laden with butter, chiefly in firkins, issued from the market-yard gate, a man between the shafts, one at either wheel, two pulling behind, all noisily endeavouring to keep the cart from running amuck downhill into the river. Close behind, like chief mourners after a hearse, one might fancy, came Tim Kerin and Nan, his wife—a battered, slow-footed couple, heavily burdened with the big load of their years, white-haired, both of them, and lean as greyhounds. Heavily they shuffled along in their clumsy boots; the man with one arm across his back, the other swinging limply; the woman holding up her skirt with one hand, and gripping with the other the handle of a big empty basket; both looking fixedly over the tail-board of the cart at the few pounds of butter for which they had slaved hard for weeks, and for which, after hours of haggling, they had just received a few most precious shillings. Fixedly they watched it, and mournfully, almost, as though they were bidding it a last farewell.

They passed through the gate, straggled across the footpath, and silently watched the cart zigzag down the street, run presently along the kerb, and, amid great shouting, discharge its contents into the packing-house.

"Faith," said Tim, across his shoulder, " 'twas cliverly done. I wonder, some day, they don't break their necks." He wagged his head dubiously; Nan tucked up her skirt; the two turned their faces uphill, and set out to share their profits with the shops. The butter was gone, and sorrow go with it: 'twas a heartbreak.

Tim Kerin's share of the profits was a shining sixpence, reluctantly tendered to him by Nan, his wife, who now walked a couple of steps behind him, with eighteenpence shut tight in her hand and the remainder of the butter-money (only a shilling or two) tied fast in a cotton bag and safely stowed away in the neck of her linsey-woolsey dress. Threepence of Tim's sixpence was to buy tobacco, a penny might go in the purchase of a weekly newspaper, a penny would buy a pair of whangs (leather laces) for his boots; the penny remaining, when all those luxuries had been honestly paid for, would buy a whole tumblerful of frothing porter.

A whole tumblerful! At sight of it, with his mind's eye, Tim's lips dried and his feet went quicker over the cobble-stones.

Nan's lips were tight, her brow wrinkled. She was figuring. It would take her to be powerful cute to fill her basket with the value of eighteenpence. Och, the lot o' things she wanted: tea, sugar, bacon, a herring for the Sunday's dinner, a bit o' white bread, and—and supposing there were a penny or two over (with knowing bargaining there might be), was it likely now that Mr Murphy, the draper, would let her have cheap a yard of narrow soiled lace to go round the border of her night-caps? Twopence might do, threepence would be sure to –. Aw, glory be to goodness, did anybody ever hear of such romancin' such extravagance? Sure it was running wild her wits were! Threepence for lace indeed!

A friend stepped from behind a cart and caught Nan by the arm. What! was it pass a neighbour like that, Mrs. Kerin would do? Pass her ouldest friend, Mrs Brady, as if she was a milestone, and never pass the time of day, or tell how she sold her butter, or how the world was using herself! "Och, och, Mrs. Kerin," moaned Mrs Brady, "what have I done to ye, at all, at all?"

Nan stopped and put out her hand, then volubly began explaining; sure, sorrow the sight of Mrs Brady she had seen; sure, she never passed a neighbour without spaking; sure, 'twas walkin' along romancin' she was, figurin' in her head, seeing how far she could make the few shillings go. "An' how are you, ma'am?" asked Nan, when full pardon for her oversight had been generously given and gratefully received. "How are you, an' all your care?"

Swiftly the two old heads bobbed together; ceaselessly their tongues began to wag; freely the full tide of their softly drawling speech flowed gurgling round the little nothings of their little world.

Meanwhile, Tim, his sixpence hot in his palm, had taken a turn through the throng of the streets, had questioned his neighbours about sales and prices (just as though he were a man of stomach and capital), had spelt out the time on the big market-house clock as he stood by the town pump listening to the hoarse drone of a ballad-singer; and now, on the side-walk of Main Street, stood dreamily looking through a shop-window at a pile of newspapers which stood precariously among an array of tobacco-pipes and sweet-bottles. If he bought a paper, Tim was thinking, he would have a whole week's diversion o' nights; if he didn't buy it, he would save the price of another tumblerful o'—A heavy hand fell on his shoulder.

"Hello!" Tim," said his neighbour, Shan Grogan; "havin' a wee squint at the sugar-sticks, is it ye are?"

"Aw ay," answered Tim, turning; "aw ay! I was just lookin' at the papers there, an' wonderin' what an ojus lot o' news they give us nowadays for a penny. Enough to keep one goin' for a week. Powerful it is."

"Yis," said Shan, "it's a wonderful world. But aisy, Tim; ha' ye been to the Post lately?"

"Naw," said Tim.

"Well, look in there if you're passin', me son. The lassie that sells the stamps asked me to tell ye. Gwan quick; mebbe she'll give ye news for nothin'."

"Now, now," answered Tim; "I'm obliged to ye, Shan; I'm obliged to ye. Now, now," he repeated to himself, as he shuffled off along the pavement; "now, now. Is Shan havin' a wee joke, I wonder?" he said, and, coming to the post-office, doubtfully sidled in.

"Me name is Kerin, miss," he said to the clerk, very humbly as to one of the representatives of mighty Government itself; "Tim, for Christian; an' they tell me ye'd mebbe be havin' somethin' for me?"

The girl handed him a letter bearing the Chicago post-mark stamped in one of its bottom corners, and carrying its address thence right up to the top of the envelope. Tim bore it tenderly to the door and carefully inspected it, then took it back to the counter.

"Whose countersign might that be, miss, if ye please?" he asked, and placed his thumb over the post-mark. Humbly he asked; curtly he was answered.

"Chicago?" said Tim. "Ay, ay! I'm obliged to ye, miss—I'm obliged to ye. May the Lord be good to ye an' send ye a duke for a husband! Good-day to ye, miss," said he, then stepped out into the street with his hand deep in his pocket and the letter in his hand, and went off in search of Nan.

"It's from Padeen," he kept thinking to himself, as he walked joyfully along, his feet clattering loosely on the pavement, his old face turning here and there, watching for his wife; "it's from Padeen, sure as ever was!" Aw! but he was glad. Aw! but Nan would be glad. So long it was, ages and ages ago, since they heard from him. 'Twasn't Padeen's hand-write—naw! but sure it might have altered; everything altered in the Big Country. Ay! 'twas only poor ould Ireland that kept the same—never any worse, never any better. But where was Nan? Sure, she ought to be in the shops. He was dying to find her. Up and down he went; at last found her, still bobbing heads at the top of Bridge Street with her friend, Mrs Brady.

"Aw, it's here ye are, Nan?" he said, coming up. "An' me huntin' the town for ye. It's yourself is well, Mrs Brady, I'm hopin'? That's right, that's right."

His voice came strangely broken and shrill; his eyes danced like a child's; still his hand gripped the letter in his pocket.

"What's the matter, Tim?" whispered Nan. "Ha' ye heard news?"

"Ay, ay," he said. "Come away till I tell ye; come away."

He turned, and, with Nan at his heels, set off almost at a run down-hill towards the river. Aw, but his heart was thumpin'!

"Aisy, Tim," cried Nan, behind him; "aisy, man, or me breath—me breath."

Without answering, or slackening his pace, Tim went on, turned through the butter-market gate, crossed the empty yard, came to the furthermost corner of one of the long, low sheds, and there halted, with his face to the wall. Aw! but his heart was thumpin'. Presently, Nan came to him, panting and flurried.

"What is it, Tim?" she asked; "what is it?"

Slowly Tim brought out his letter, and, holding it by both hands, let his wife look at it.

"It's—it's from Padeen!" cried she; "it's from Padeen!"

"Yis," said Tim. "It's not his hand-write, but it must be from him."

"Aw, glory be to God!" cried Nan. "Glory to God! Sure, it's ages since we heard from the boy, ages!"

She put down her basket, and, with her head between Tim's shoulder and the wall, looked fixedly at the envelope. Aw! but she was glad to see it. Such a time it was since they had heard from Padeen! A whole two years it was, come Christmas, since the last letter came, with that money-order in it, an' the beautiful picture of Padeen himself, dressed out in his grand clothes, with a gold chain across his waistcoat, and a gold ring on his finger. A whole two years almost. And now maybe—?

"Aw, Tim, open it quick," she panted; "open it quick!"

"Mebbe," said Tim, "we'd better wait till we get home. The light's bad, an'"

"No, no, Tim; no, no; it'd kill me to wait."

"Ay!" said Tim, then slowly drew his knife from his pocket and tenderly cut open the top of the envelope. His fingers trembled greatly as he fumbled with the enclosure. Nan's hand went quick to her heart.

"Aw, quick, Tim!" she cried. "Quick, quick!"

"Don't—don't flooster me, woman," said Tim. "I can't—can't—" The next moment his shaking old fingers held a sheet of note-paper, and a black-edged card on which, in large letters, beneath a long silvern cross, were the words: PATRICK KERIN.

Nan fell back a step; her fingers clutched at her dress over her heart Tim's knife clattered upon the stones, and the envelope fluttered down. For a while they stood there silent, dread-stricken. At last Nan spoke.

"Read, Tim," she said. "Read!"

"I—I can't."

"Ye must, Tim; it's better. Let us know the worst, for God's sake! Read, Tim."

"I—I—" Tim began; then quickly opened the sheet. "It's—it's too dark here," he mumbled. "I—I want me specs."

"Read what ye can, Tim, an' quick, for God's sake!"

So Tim, still with his face to the wall, raised the letter to catch the light, and began to read:

Chicago City, U. S. A.

Dear—dear Mister Kerin—*It is my—my sad duty to inform you that your son Patrick died* ("Aw, Padeen, Padeen!") *ofty—typhus here on the third of this month at twelve o' clock a.m.,* ("God's mercy!" cried Nan.) *As his oldest friend, I was with him at the end. He died in peace. He was buried at his request, in— Cemetery, I, I send you something to—to keep"* . . .

"Aw, I can read no more," said Tim with a groan; "it's too dark. I can read no more. Me poor ould Padeen!"

Nan turned and looked vacantly across at the busy street, dry-eyed and gray-faced. Ah! her poor Padeen, dead and buried away among the strangers, dead and buried, and never, never would she see him again, never hear his voice, never grip his hand! Dead, dead! her big, handsome, noble son....

She turned to Tim and caught him by the sleeve.

"Come away, Tim," she said. "Come away wi' me." Tim looked at her.

"Aw! Nan, Nan," he said, as the big tears sprang to his eyes. "Nan, me girl, but it's hard!"

"Aw, yis," said she, and lifted her basket; "but come away, Tim, come away. Home's the best place for us."

"Yis," said Tim, wiping his eyes with his hand. "Yis, Nan;" then, Nan leading the way, and Tim shuffling after, the two old people (mourners now in real earnest) crossed the yard; and at the gate Nan halted.

"I think," said she, as Tim came up, "I think we can manage this week wi'out the bits o' groceries. Sure, they're only luxuries, anyway. I'll go an' see if Mr Murphy can find me a bit o' crape for me bonnet."

"Do," said Tim. "Do, Nan; an' when you're about it," he said, taking his sixpence from his pocket and handing it to her, "ye may as well get me a bit for me hat. Ay! sure I can do wi'out me tabaccy for one week. Aw! Away quick, Nan; an' hurry back, me girl."

So Nan turned up towards the market-house; but Tim went downhill towards the bridge; and when, presently, Nan came to him, carrying her little packet of crape in her big basket, Tim's head was bowed over the parapet, and he was mumbling tearfully. "Aw, me poor Padeen, me poor Padeen!"

Nan plucked at his sleeve.

"Come away home, Tim," she said, "come away!" And at the word Tim raised his head, dried his eyes, and set off slowly after Nan up the long, dusty road that wearily led towards home.

THE EMIGRANT

She leant out of the carriage window and saw the van-door close; then called to the porter if her box were safe and sound.

"Aw, ay," said he, and slouched up, wiping the wet from his hand on his corduroys; "aw, ay; it'll follow ye safe to Clogheen, anyhow. Good-bye, an' God speed ye!"

"Good-bye," she said, and gave him her hand. "But aren't the rest o' ye comin'?" she called.

The station-master came and gave her a parting word; then two or three town loiterers; then the station-master's wife, with a shawl over her head, and picking her way through the puddles; last of all came a man—the girl's father, one could see—running stiffly, and glancing back often at the horse and cart standing forlorn outside the gate.

"Good-bye, Mary," he said, "an' God be with ye, me girl." He held her hand for a second or two and his lips kept moving whilst she answered bravely. "Ye'll write from New York?"

"I will—aw, at once."

"Do—don't keep us waitin'," he said; then stood back with the others, and blinked at the driving rain. She pulled a handkerchief from a battered brown hand-bag, and nervously wiped her lips.

"Ah," called she, "ye all thought yes'd see me cryin'. Ah, I tricked ye rightly."

"Ah, no," answered the porter; "we knew ye'd be brave."

"Ay, ay," assented the rest, and shifted their legs; "ay, ay."

"Away ye go," shouted the guard; the engine shrieked; Mary shook out her handkerchief and called good-bye; her friends waved an arm; she had started for the States.

"They thought I'd cry," said she, as she sat back and fell to plucking at the fingers of her woollen gloves. "They thought I'd cry—och, no!"

She was brave; yet her lips were quivering, and her eyes were turned mournfully on the fields and hedges and the cottages here and there shining white through the grey drift of the rain.

"We'll soon be at it," she said presently. "Ah, Lord, the day it is! An' the state I'm in; och, och." She stooped and wrung the water from her bedraggled skirt. "An' me hair that tattered; aw, it's shockin'! But I didn't cry," she said, and flashed her black eyes at me. "Och, no. Whisht! We're getting' near it. Aw, there it is; there they are! Good-bye, *muther!* Good-bye, *Patsey* an' *Johnny* an' *Lizzie!* Good-bye *all!*"

I stood up, and over her hat caught a glimpse of the group gathered on the street before the cottage: the mother in her night-cap, the children bare-legged, all waving their arms and caps, and crying their farewells.

"Good-bye," cried Mary back through the rain; "och, good-bye!"

That was the last of them she would see, she said, as she sat down again, the last, till the Lord knew when. She was for the States? asked some one. Ah, she was; she could get work there; she could do nothing at home. Sure, it was better to go than to be a burden on them all. Ah, yes; she had been out before an' had come home to settle, but—but, and her handkerchief went fast to her lips—well, things had turned out troublesome. She'd do better out there; there were too many at home, and her mother was poorly. Ah, an', sure times were shockin' bad.

"Ay, ay," the men went in chorus; "they are, they are;" then looked mournfully at her red cheeks, and from one to another passed the word that she was a brave girl, so she was; a brave girl; and God speed her, said they, as one by one they went out clumsily at Glann station, and left Mary and me together.

It was fair-day at Glann; therefore did the train settle itself by the platform for a long rest. "The guard mebbe's gone to see the fair," said Mary; and I laughed, stamped vigorously (for it was cold) across the carriage floor, wiped the window, and looked out.

Down the further bank of the railway, along a narrow path which had started beyond the fields somewhere near the town, was coming a little procession of six men, bearing a coffin on a rough hurdle made of ash poles. The men were bare-headed; a single bunch of wild flowers lay atop the streaming coffin; there were no mourners, nor anywhere could one see any sign of sorrow or curiosity. They came on down, the men with their pitiful burden, crossed a track, came to a siding, slid the coffin into a fish-van, shut the door, pulled their soft felt hats from their pockets, mopped their faces, then took shelter behind the van and lit their pipes.

There wanted only a bottle to make the scene complete, and I was confidently watching for it, when right at my elbow arose a great sobbing.

"Aw, aw," cried Mary; "did ye see? Did ye see? Och! what a way to be tr'ated! An' such a day for a buryin'! All out in the wet—the wet an' the cowld. Aw, poor crature! Aw, muther, muther, ye'll die, ye'll die! I'll niver see ye again, nor father, nor no one. Aw, it's cruel to lave ye. I'll go back; I'll go back!"

Her sobs were pitiful. Loiterers began to gather round the door. It was only a poor girl going to America, I explained; they would pity her, I was sure. Ah, they would, said they, and went, all but one: a big, sunburnt fellow dressed in rough tweed, who came forward and asked my leave. For what? Ah, he knew the girl; came in, went over and laid a rough hand on Mary's shoulder.

"Ah, don't," she said. "I'll go home, I'll go home."

"What ails ye, Mary, at all?" said he, and shook her again.

She turned. "Ah, God A'mighty, James!" she cried; and her tears went. "It's you. Where are ye goin'? What brings ye? Who towld ye?"

James sat down heavily, and began beating his boot with his stick. Ah, he'd been to the fair, had sold early, was waiting for a train to take him home.

"Where are ye goin'?" he said over his shoulder. "What wur ye bleartin' about?"

Mary hung her head and did not answer.

"Where are ye goin'?" he said again.

She looked up at him quickly, almost defiantly. "To the States."

He nodded; began again the tattoo on his boot; and before another word came the train had started.

"We're goin'," said Mary. "Hurry an' say good-bye, or they'll shut ye in."

"No matter," he answered; "I'll stay where I am."

The maid sat apart from the man, and answered his abrupt, mannerless questions as bravely as she might

Why was she going? Ah, he knew; there was no need to ask.

Why had she not told him? Better not; what was the use? All was over between them.

The man eyed her wonderingly. Over? he repeated. Over? Did she not know he was ready to make it up, and—to do his best? Ay, yes, she knew; still —

Still, what? It was better to go, she said, and looked tearfully out at the flying fields.

Yes, it was better to go; I agreed with Mary. He was a lout, for certain; a good-for-nothing, by all chance. She would lose nothing by leaving him. There, there, sitting beside her, was the trouble about which she had spoken. She had come home to settle down with him; but things had been troublesome. Ah, yes. One knew it all. He had been easy-going and lazy; wanted things to turn up, felt no inclination to hurry into married cares. Aw, sure, he could wait awhile; and if he, then Mary. Something like that it had been; anyhow, Mary had not settled. They had quarrelled, and now she was leaving him for better or worse. She was wise. Had the man no bowels? Had he nothing for her but hard questions and pitying looks? Would he not, before he went, say one kind word to this girl who had trusted in his word and manhood, and finding them wanting was now leaving him for ever? Did there not some golden memory linger about his heart? Not one. He was wooden to the core. He would sit on there, tapping his boot and staring at his big freckled hands, neither hurt nor sorry, but just wondering that a girl could be such a fool; the train would stop, and with a nod and a flabby shake of the hand, he would take himself out into the rain. And good riddance!

The train slowed; Mary's lips began to quiver. The train stopped; I gathered in my legs, so that the fellow might pass without touching me. He raised his head and looked out at the sky.

"Ah, I may as well g' wan to the junction," he drawled; "it'll be all the same; one could do nothin' such a day, anyhow."

"Yis," said Mary, and not cheerlessly. "Sure, ye may as well."

We sat silent all the way to Clogheen, and there we parted: Mary, so it was set down, to catch a train North, James one back home, and I to do my work in the town.

Two hours afterwards I met the two in the rain-swept streets, and in my surprise stopped short before them. Mary looked up and laughed.

"Ah," said she, "I'm here yit; that train went without me."

"Oh," said I; "that's very bad; why, the next won't be here for hours. And you're drenched? But—but" and I looked at James as he stood, slightly flushed and dripping wet, blankly staring across the street.

"Ah, yis," Mary answered. "James missed his, too; I'm not goin' at all; sure, we've made it up."

I put my watch slowly back into my pocket and nodded.

"James has promised me," she went on, and her eyes fell; "an' we're goin' to get marr'ed come harvest-time; an' he'll try hard for a place at the big house above. An'—an'—God knows, Sir, I'm not sorry, for me heart was sore at lavin' home."

They knew their own business best; but there fell an awkward silence, so I asked James concerning his prospects. Did he see his way clearly?

Ah, he did; and began tapping his boots. Sure, there was always a way if one could only wait till it came. "Isn't she better here, anyway, whatever comes," said he, and gave me a moment's glimpse at his face, "than out yonder wid the strangers? Sure, 'twas madness av her to think o' it; sure. Providence sent me to Glann fair."

Providence? And had Providence sent also that dismal procession to the fish-van, that Mary might see it and sob for her friends, and her James, and the home of her heart?

"And you, Mary?" I asked. "Are you quite satisfied?"

"Ah, yis," said she mournfully. "Ah, I hope so."

I took her into a shop and bought her a little wedding gift—a silver brooch, shaped like a harp and set with green marble, then wished them more happiness than I ever hoped they would have, and went my way.

Three hours afterwards saw me at Clogheen station again, and there was Mary, standing dejected by her little yellow box.

"Not gone home yet, Mary?" I asked.

Her handkerchief fluttered out.

"No-o, Sir. I—was lookin' for ye. I—I wanted to give ye back this;" and she held out the brooch. "I'll niver wear it. Och, it's all over. I—I'm goin' on to catch the ship."

It was well. I determined that this time neither Providence nor emotion should hinder her going.

"Ah, no," she sobbed; "'twas only foolishness. Me heart was sore at lavin' them all; an' the sight o' that coffin an' James comin' like that—Och, I cudn't bear it! But 'twas foolish av me; it's better for me to go."

I took the brooch, pinned it on her jacket, and spoke a foolish word or two by way of comfort. She would, I hoped, wear it for my sake, if not for . . .

"Aw, Sir," she burst out, "if he'd only been *steady*! for I liked him well. Och, och!"

She turned and looked down the platform; there sat James, drunk and asleep.

SHAN'S DIVERSION

Market-day and its glories were over; all about the Grogan's home was snug for the night; Shan and Biddy sat on stools by the hearth-stone, silently enjoying their supper of a toasted herring and white bread and tea.

Suddenly Shan slapped his knee, set his bowl on the floor, and, after a deal of fumbling, brought forth a letter from the inner pocket of his waist-coat.

"Niver crossed me mind t' this mortial minute," he began apologetically; "if it hadn't come into me head about meetin' Phil, the lad in the post-office, I'd niver."

"Who's it from?" snapped Biddy.

Shan looked sideways at the envelope. Well, that was hard to say just yet, he thought; but the lassie in the office told him it came from America, so he supposed—

"Whisht, ye fool!" cried his wife. "It's from yir brother Mike. Open it quick."

Shan took out his clasp-knife, cautiously slit the envelope, and pulled out half a sheet of notepaper carefully folded over a money order.

"Give uz it," said Biddy, as she shot out her crooked fingers. "No—th' other—the money. How much is it?"

"How can I tell till I read it? Aisy, till I see what th' ould boy says."

Shan shifted his stool till he had brought his back against the chimney-jamb; then leant towards the fire to catch its light. The letter was short and quite matter of fact: the writer was well, requested an answer, enclosed a trifle to help with the rent.

"That's the whole av it, ivery scrape," said Shan. "Well, thank God, the ould boy's in health —"

"Give uz it," said Biddy, sharply; "an' read this. Tell uz quick."

Shan took the order, leant again towards the firelight, and from the very first word began to spell out its contents. Presently he came to the kernel of the matter: "the sum of—T-w-o pounds?"

Like a flash came the temptation—a temptation which at any time might have come to Shan, as to any honest man, but which just then, thanks to the malignant potency of market-day whisky, he was hardly prepared to resist.

"T-w-o, T-w-o—" he stammered. There were ten shillings more: suppose he did not read them? Biddy would be none the wiser, and he could. . .

"Ach! what ails ye, stammerin' an' stutterin' lek that?" said Biddy, querulously.

"Och! It's the light," said Shan, and shifted his stool; "shure it's ojus bad."

"Only two pound," said Biddy. "Give it over—I've heard enough."

Shan reached the money order to his wife: Fate had willed it; two pounds he had read, the rest, only for Biddy, he might have read: two pounds then it must remain.

He put his head back against the jamb, closed his eyes, and began to think. His mind was a little confused, his moral sense a little dulled (as indeed sometimes happens with the natives of Bilboa on market-days); still certain broad facts stood clear against the feeble flow of his thought.

He had lied—yes; but maybe he'd have told the truth had she let him read on. The lie might pass . . . The two pounds were Biddy's; yes, every farthing of them. Ay! but the ten shillings were his—if he could get them.

Could he? . . . Ten shillings! Since he married, never once had he had so much to call his own—not once. Whatever he sold—pigs, calves, potatoes, all the money went to Biddy—Biddy—Biddy! Was that how a man should be treated? Well, please God, some day he'd make a change; he'd show his teeth. He didn't care a curse about money—still, he was treated hard . . . And now! yes, be damned to him! but he'd have that ten shillings if he had to go on his knees to Bunn for it.

His face flushed with a spurious courage; he looked cautiously across at Biddy. With her elbows set on her knees, she sat forward, thinking hard, and sometimes mumbling as she looked over the top of the money order into the fire.

Upstairs, in a safe place between the thatch and the side-wall, was hidden the pound or two which hitherto had made the whole fortune of the Grogans. This God-send, so Biddy was thinking, added to that hoard, more than doubled it,—a powerful lot of money to be under the roof with two lone people! . . . Ah! it was all needed sore. A new pair of corduroys for Shan; a striped shawl for herself; a—a—naw! the bonnet must go. They wanted a skillet, a gallon, and a milking porringer . . . Could she get that bonnet? Och, och! her wits were wandering ... And the rent? Aw! the rent might go to glory. She'd pay when she was made, not a foot sooner. And—and who knew what might turn up? Maybe another order!

She looked at the piece of white paper between her hands. To think that meant two POUNDS. Two whole pounds! It looked shocking thin and delicate. Suppose she lost it, tore it? Suppose the post-office smashed and couldn't pay? Aw! Aw!

Almost fiercely she turned to Shan. "We'll start for Bunn first thing in the mornin'," said she. "D'ye hear me?"

Shan turned on his stool and began rubbing his ear. Sure the divil was in the woman—send him alone! If she came, sign for and draw all the money—ji'—

"D'ye hear me?" repeated Biddy.

"All right," said Shan. "All right. Jist as ye lek."

It was not all right, though, and the knowledge kept Shan that night awake for hours. Where was his Dutch courage now? Gone with the snuffing of the candle. It was as certain that

Biddy would go to Bunn and find him out as that she was lying even then in the bed beside him. Oh! he wished the ten shillings in the pit of hell! ... Confess? Naw—naw—he dare not! Better trust to luck—maybe something would turn up.

Nothing turned up in the night; nothing the next morning; nothing all that weary way to Bunn. Shan's heart was heavy as his unwilling feet. Never had the streets given him a colder welcome. And there was the post-office; and nothing had turned up. Well! so be it.

What was that? He must sign his name? Indeed; and where? There!

Aw, very well. Give him grip of a pen. Something flashed upon him ... Yes! He'd try. He squared his elbows, cocked his head, dabbed the pen down viciously—and broke it. Ach! such pens. Was that the best her Majesty's Government could do? He tried another—it broke. Well, sorrow take the like he ever came across! Couldn't write of course he could. What! they had no more! He drew a penny from his pocket, threw it on the counter, and implored Biddy to do a charity and go next door for a ha'porth o' nibs. Biddy hesitated; could see no harm in going; went, and presently returning met Shan in the post-office doorway with two sovereigns in his outstretched palm.

"Ha!" said he, "shure I shamed them. Ye wur hardly out o' the dure when they rowled out the finest pens ye iver seen—ay, by the dozen. An' there's yir money safe as the Bank."

So far very well. But soon for Shan arose this question: What should he do with the half sovereign, which just then lay wrapped in paper at the root of a great thistle in the corner of a field? He could not bank it; his fear of Biddy forbade that he should carry it, or spend it, or hide it in the house. It was worth less than nothing lying there fallow; some morning, stealthy as his visits were, Biddy would surely discover him gloating over his treasure; he might die and leave it to the worms and the jingle of a stranger's spade. Yes, thought Shan, as he stood, one fine May morning, leaning on his shovel in a potato farrow; yes, something must be done with it. It haunted his sleep, puckered his brow, was a load on his mind, was the divil's own bother entirely.

From far away, across the hills, came a shrill whistle, and, quick after it, the rumble of the first morning train on its way from Clogheen to Bunn. For the hundredth time Shan wished that he could have just one jaunt by steam right out into the wonders of the world. What! . . . Yes, by thunder! There was the money waiting at the thistle root. He hadn't had a day's diversion since his wedding-day—twenty long years ago.... Biddy! Pah! He would be a man for once; he'd go. Yes, but perhaps, after all, it were best to go peacefully and knowingly.

All day long he pondered. Five o'clock came and Biddy's Hoi-i-i from the hill. He drove the point of his shovel under a root, bore hard on the handle, smashed the metal across, and with the broken pieces in his hand went sadly up to tea.

Dear, oh dear! such a misfortune—broke it at the last shovelful. And there was the field only half done, and he hadn't another. Borrow one! Of course not, and everybody busy like himself. A spade? Did Biddy say a spade might do? Aw, 'deed it might, and so might a wooden spoon if the nights were all days! Get a new one! Ay! he supposed so; there was no other way out of it; that was the way the money went; och, och, all that long tramp into Bunn! Go then! Go that night?

"Is it walk to Bunn an' back now ye'd have me do?" Shan asked with a world of reproach in his voice. "Now, after all that day's work? Be the King! but it's worse than digger drivin'."

Well, then, could he be back early in the morning?

"Mebbe," said Shan, "mebbe; if the shops is open mebbe I cud." He stretched himself lazily; put on his hat; went out, and turning into the burre there covered his mouth with his hand and silently laughed.

Early next morning, Shan, with the price of a new shovel in his pocket, left home and started for Bunn. He kept to the road for about half a mile; then doubled back through the fields and rescued his half sovereign from the thistle root.

Once on the road again his spirits rose with a bound. From the mountains the air came fresh as dew; the hedges were alive with birds singing among the young green.

"She dressed me up in scarlet-red!" trotted Shan in his glee, "an' treated me very kindly.

But still I thought me heart've break for the girl I left behind me?"

The girl he left behind him? Biddy!—Biddy befooled and beguiled at home! Ho! Ho! He put his hands on his knees and laughed down at the road.

Only a shop here and there in Bunn was open. The air was heavy with fresh peatsmoke. Slatternly women came to the doors and blinked at Shan; their husbands, lounging and smoking against the walls, gave him good-day. He answered shortly and quickened his pace. His mind was quite fixed that, whatever befell, Bunn town should see nothing of his diversion. So, keeping his face firmly from the public houses, he walked steadily up the gold tight in his hand made straight for the railway station. He would take the train to Clogheen and there divert himself. He would have a good dinner, two bottles of stout—not a drop more, not one; buy a red pocket-handkerchief for himself and a new night-cap for Biddy; take the one o'clock train back, buy his shovel, go straight home and take meekly whatever might come.

Heavens above! what a day he would have! The grandest for twenty long years: a whole day to himself—plenty of money—a good dinner—By the King!

He was passing the fair green and in sight of the station. A whistle sounded; he began to run; whoof! whoof! went the engine: Shan had missed his train.

He sat down on the ditch and mopped his face. Och, och! the poor luck he had. What could he do? The next train did not start till mid-day—och, och! What could he do? go home and toil all day? He pulled his hat off, and with an oath dashed it on the road. The morning freshness had sped; not a bird sang in the hedges; the sky above laughed savagely down. Go back home! Leave diversion behind and drudge through a whole weary day! One minute late, only one. Ah! might the divil swamp the train.

He rose, picked up his hat, and feeling almost inclined to beat his disappointed head against the wall, made for the town . . . One minute late—one—one . . . The bottles in the window of the hotel parlour caught his eye and gleamed comfort upon him; he stopped, hesitated, went to the door, turned back, turned again and went with a rush through the doorway.

An hour went and left Shan lighter in pocket and head; the second saw him waxed fervid, shouting patriotism, wisdom, treason across the table at his friend the town butcher. Another friend or two joined them. Ah! he was the boy knew a trifle; he was the boy knew how to treat a friend; name their drink, name their drink!

By this, only for fate, Shan's diversion in Clogheen would have been in full swing. Biddy at home was expecting him. Ah! divil cared; more whisky there! Another hour passed.

Shan's head was reeling; his mood verging on the quarrelsome. The butcher gave him the lie; got it back; answered brutally. Shan rose to fight, and the next moment was out in the street storming at the door.

A crowd flew together. Shan evened his arms and appealed for justice. He had been robbed, insulted. "Aw yis", thought Bunn town, "aw yis, an' so do lots more get insulted when they take drink on an empty stomach. An' Shan Grogan of all men, too! an easygoin' harmless—whisht! The police! . . . Run, Shan run! . . . Run, Shan; we're for ye, me boy!"

Shan stood firm. The police were the men he wanted. He had been insulted, robbed.

"Go hame," they said; did they say? What! they refused to hear him? They refused to see justice done? Ah! the bloodthirsty renegades! the black-hearted cut-throats! . . . Let them dare touch him! Whew-w-w! he defied them!

Bunn town cheered Shan as the police closed. He hit out right and left; then broke through the warring crowd and made downhill towards the river.

"Run, Shan; run, ye boy, ye," cried Bunn; and backed its voice by repeated efforts to stop the career of the law. No use! Reinforcements hurried out; the handcuffs were as good as on Shan's wrists. He reached the bridge panting and weary. Suddenly he reeled and fell heavily against the parapet. Behind him were the police, angry and remorseless; before him stood a woman with her hands raised and her face big with horror and surprise.

The police ran on; Bunn town stopped dead.

"Aw! aw!" went up the voices. "Aw! aw! Be the Lord, but it's Biddy!"

Well, when a man hits the police he pays for his sport; and Shan Grogan may thank his luck, and the tearful pleading of his wife, and the eager testimony of his friends and neighbours, that the price he paid for the one diversion of his married life was no more than a night in the cells, and all but a shilling or two of the little hoard which many months of striving (and the kindness of a brother) had gathered between the side-wall and the thatch of his little cottage in Bilboa.

THE SPLENDID SHILLING

I

"Please, Mr John," said Mary the servant, "Master's sent me for ye. He's above in the front parlour."

"What does he want?" asked Mr John, and raised his eyes. "Tell him I'm busy."

"I did, Sir. I said the mower was bruk an' ye wur fixin' it; but he only roared at me. I'd go, Mr John; 'deed I wid."

"What the sorrow now?" said John, and put down his wrench on the stones of the yard. "Roared ye say, Mary?"

"Ay! Och, Sir, spake him fair; don't anger him worse. I know what ails him. Her mother was here a while ago—it's that, Mr John."

"Ay," said John, and his face darkened. "Ay! An' what the devil brought her here?"

He rose from his knees, turned down his shirt-sleeves over his brown arms, then took his sleeved waistcoat from the pole of the mowing machine and buttoned it on. "Did she stay long, Mary?" asked he.

"No, Sir; only a wee while—but I heerd words."

"Ay," said John, and turned towards the kitchen door of the farmhouse. "Oh, just so!"

"Ye'll spake him fair, Mr John," said Mary the servant, and ventured to lay her hand on his arm. "Och, ye will, Sir! Ye know, I'd—we'd be sorry to lose ye, Sir."

John hung on his heel for a step, and looked down at his little well-wisher standing bare-headed and bare-footed in her rags and tatters.

"Oh, ay," he said, and laughed. "Oh, ay! Never fear, Mary; I'll speak him fair, true an' fair as a die. An' I'm thankful to you, my girl, for the hint ye gave me; it's as well to know."

Then his face fell solemn again; and, with his hands clasped across his back, he went in through the kitchen and along the red-flagged hall into the front parlour.

James Hewitt was sitting in an old leather arm-chair reading from a newspaper. A man of about sixty-five years he was, grey-headed, swarthy, large-limbed, strong of face, a fine type of your Ulster Protestant farmer, and the living image of what you would expect his son John to be when Time had added another forty or so to the sum of his years.

"Ye wanted me?" asked John, from his place by the door, where he stood fumbling with his cap.

His father lowered his newspaper and looked at him over the rims of his spectacles; then raised the sheet again as if to read.

"Yes," answered he, "I did. You'd better sit down."

"I'd rather stand. I'm waitin'"

Both the words and the manner in which they were spoken were disrespectful; very seldom had child of his dared venture so to speak in the presence of James Hewitt. For once, however, the words passed unrebuked.

"Have ye mended that machine?" came from behind the newspaper.

"No; nor won't. Is that all?"

Clearly John foresaw a storm, and was for brewing it at once. His father threw down his paper and sat forward in his chair.

"Won't; won't!" cried he, wrathfully. "What do ye mean, Sir? Have ye come here to defy me?"

"That's as maybe. I meant I couldn't mend it."

"Then why didn't ye say so?"

"It's no odds. I'm waitin', I say. I know what I'm here for, so ye may as well say your say at once."

The two men eyed each other for a moment, straight and steadily: along the deep lines of the father's face anger was swiftly flushing; in John's eyes obstinacy was fast seated.

"Oh, ye know, do ye?" the father began; then all suddenly broke out: "How dare ye disobey me, Sir? Didn't I tell ye, last time I spoke to ye about this, that ye were to give up your—your foolishness wi'—wi' that hussy over there? Didn't I, Sir?"

"Ye did."

"Well?"

"Well, I didn't choose to obey ye. Why should I? A man can do as he likes, I suppose?" Suddenly John made a step from the door, "Look here, father," said he, and his voice came low and solemn; "let's be plain an' have done, for God's sake! It goes against me to be doin' what ye don't like, but that can't be helped. Ye asked me to give up Rachel Hoey, an' to have no more to say to her. Well, I haven't given her up, because I couldn't; an' I won't give her up, because I can't; so help me

God! Ye may say your worst an' do it; but there's my say as plain as I can put it."

The young man put his back against the door, folded his arms, and so standing, with his eyes steadily fixed on the wall before him, waited for the words of his fate. Very soon they came, swiftly, wrathfully, gathering force at every sentence. James Hewitt was obliged to his son for his plain speaking, and dutiful conduct, and grateful reward for all that had been done for him. It was always pleasant for a father to find his children thwarting and defying him, and insulting his grey hairs.

"I don't want to defy ye, Sir," said John, and spoke more dutifully than he had yet done; "an' I don't think I've insulted ye."

"But ye have, Sir," his father went on; "ye have insulted me, spoke to me like a plough-boy. By God, Sir, for two pins I'd flog ye!"

John smiled. "It's too late for that now," said he; "those days are past."

"Ay! They're past, ye think," cried the old man; "they're past, an' so ye defy me. But they're not past, I tell ye; I'm master in my own house yet, thank God! An' if I can't strap ye I can sack ye. Ye hear that? I told ye before what I'd do. I said if ye had any more doin's wi' them Hoeys, if ye didn't keep from their house, if ye didn't renounce the arts o' that little jade, I'd . . ."

"She's no jade, father," said John, quietly. "Even from you I'll not hear that."

"But ye will hear it, Sir. Ye knew, I told ye myself, that no Hoey'd ever call himself my friend, that between them an' me there was never, an' never could be, anything but hatred.

They're a pack o' rogues an' liars, one an' all; there never was one o' them yet fit to carry rags to a beggarman. An' yet—yet ye tell me ye'll marry that jade? Yes, jade! An' ye send her mother to me here to speak for ye—"

"I didn't send her," said John; "I knew nothing of it."

"She came; that's enough. I want to hear no more. An' now you come, an' forgetful o' all I've done for ye, ye ungrateful scoundrel! Ye say ye'll defy me an' keep on wi' your devices; that ye will do what ye like; that ye will marry this girl; that ye don't care for what I say. Don't ye? Look ye here, John, here's a plain word for ye. Are ye or are ye not goin' to do my biddin'?"

"Ye mean give Rachel up?"

"I do."

"No."

"Then out ye go. I disown ye. From this day you're no son o' mine. Ye hear?"

"I do."

"I'll curse the day ye were born. I'll cut ye off wi' a shillin'. Wait!"

The old man rose from his chair, crossed the room, and opening a safe which stood in the corner, took therefrom a folded paper.

"Ye see that?" he cried, and faced his son once more. "Ye see that? It's my will, an' in it I've left ye all I possess. Well," and he took the paper between both hands, "here's your chance. Take back your word an' it stands; say the word an' I flitter it. Come!"

"Flitter," said John; and the will went fluttering over the floor.

"It's the last o' ye," shouted James. "Take yourself off! I disown ye. Out o' my sight, An' this house!"

But John stood calm, with his back against the door, and his arms still folded.

"Very well," said he, and the words came slowly as from a tongue striving for calmness.

"Very well, I'll go. An' may neither o' us rue this day. But I'll say this —"

"Ye'll say nothin'. My solemn curse on ye. Out ye go!"

John stepped forward.

"But I will speak, father," said he; "for you're unjust. What have I done? Fell in love wi' a girl. What do I want? Only to marry her. It's true ye dislike her an' hers. Well, can I help that? I wanted nothin' o' ye, only to be left alone. An' now ye curse me, disown me! Ye might ha' kept your breath to cool your porridge. I'll leave your house in welcome; an' may your curses come back to—" John stopped suddenly. "No," he went on; "I'll not say it; for cursin' is the work o' the devil. But as the word comes so I take it." He held out his hand. "Good-bye."

His father turned away.

"Ye won't shake hands? Come, father; an' may God forgive us."

But the old man said not a word; and the next moment John had turned his back on father and home.

II

John took his coat from a peg in the hall; and without more ado (without a glance, even, through the passage door into the kitchen, where all tearful stood a little bare-footed figure) went out through the front door. He was homeless now and penniless; the wide world was before him. Where should he go? He looked away across the hills, towards the place where dwelt the maid of his heart, the maid for whom he had just forgone so much.

Ah, over there was a friend awaiting him, a friend true as steel, whose own true self was worth all else in the world. All else? All else? His eyes fell on the broad acres standing before him, rich in crop, fat in pasture, dotted with horses and cattle; over there was the orchard, with the sunlight shimmering through the bending branches; close by, just beyond that hedge, was the garden all trim and gay and bountiful; behind, was the old homestead, long, white, comfortably old-fashioned. All that was his inheritance. In sight of it all he had been born and reared; it was his every acre, every stone of it—only for Rachel.

"Is she worth it all? Is she worth it all?" he asked himself, as, turning, he made straight down the lawn, and coming presently to a newly mown meadow, there flung himself on the fresh, cool grass. "Is she worth it all?" he repeated over and over. Yes, yes, his heart answered, she is worth it all, worth the whole world to you, John Hewitt.... Was he doing wisely? Would it not have been better to have taken Mary the servant's advice, to have spoken his father fairly, to have thrown himself on his forbearance and forgiveness; at least not so entirely to have ruined his chances? He had acted impulsively, obstinately. Yes, yes; but what other way was there? Wild horses would not move his father; he hated the Hoeys like poison; you might as well ask tears from a tombstone as forgiveness from James Hewitt. No, no; there was no other way; his bed was made and he must lie on it; for weal or woe the world was before him empty of all but his own self and that little girl over there beyond the hilltops. Ah, but she was everything, everything; a bonnie lass, the pride of his heart. She was everything; let him go seek comfort and consolation at her hands.

With this great yearning for sympathy close at his heart, John, about nightfall, set out across the Gorteen country, and, in a while, came to a thatched farmhouse set low in the hollow of the hills. A garden, enclosed by a painted fence and full (just then in the peaceful gloaming) of the heavy odours of old-fashioned cottage flowers, lay in front; and at the gate, soberly clad in a fresh print gown, stood Rachel. Her face lit up at sound of his step and at sight of his wished-for face; surely a bonnie lass was she, bright-eyed, rosy-cheeked—a bright vision, you would have said, for any disconsolate lover cast out into the hollow of an empty world. John quickened his stride along the grass path by the orchard hedge; and with his hands out came soon to the little gate, and his sweet-heart standing there waiting for his greeting. Ah, how glad he was to see her, to hear her voice; never before had her face shone out more winsome, or her hand clasped his with a warmer pressure of welcome! His heart was full of a great thankfulness for the gift of her dear presence and love. Ah, it was great, great; worth all the world, that moment there with Rachel in his arms!

Presently he took her hand, led her into the orchard, and there, under the spreading branches of an old apple-tree, sat down beside her.

"Well, Rachy," said he, all suddenly, "it's come at last."

"What, John?"

"The word to go. Father an' myself had a talk this mornin'. We—we—'Twas an angry scene."

"Oh, John!"

"Ay, Rachy, my girl, the world's before us. I've nothin' now in the world but you, acusbla; only you, my girl. But it's enough, isn't it, Rachy? Eh? Isn't it?"

Rachel dropped her eyes and began twisting her ring round her finger.

"Yes, John," answered she, "I suppose so. But you'll tell me about this affair wi' your Father? Who—how did it begin?"

Then John, without referring, just then, to the unfortunate visit Mrs Hoey had paid to his father that day (a visit which, as he well knew, Rachel had neither prompted nor encouraged, but which was simply the well-meant manoeuvre of an anxious mother), and without much exaggeration, for John was a modest man, and no artist in the science of words, told his sweet-heart the story of his interview with his father, its beginning, progress, disastrous close. "It was to be," said John; "it was to be. I knew surely when Mary—when I set foot inside the parlour and saw his face that it was all over wi' me. It's been comin' for months; didn't I tell him, months back, Rachel, that I wouldn't give ye up, an' didn't he know the kind o' me? He was only waitin' to see what I'd do. What kind is he at all?"

"Oh, it's all a mistake," cried Rachel; and John, not heeding, went on.

"What kind is he?" asked he, and spread his hands. "How could he do such a thing? His own flesh an' blood? Turn me out, disown his own son! For what? Because I chose my own wife for myself; because I, a grown man, refused to do his biddin'; because you an' yours weren't to his likin'. An' to curse me—curse me, his own flesh an' blood! Ah, may God repay . . .!"

Rachel caught his arm with both hands.

"No, no, John," cried she. "No, no! I'm not worth that."

"But ye are," answered John, his wrath suddenly falling, "ye are, acusbla; worth all in the world. Never heed, my lass, never heed; let the curses go an' all else wi' them. I've got you, Rachey. Eh, Rachey? I've got you, an' you've got me; an' together we'll face the world. Won't we, deary? Look at me, Rachel; look at me. Ye do care for me?"

Rachel looked up frankly at him.

"Ye needn't ask that, John," said she. "Ye know I'd go to the ends o' the earth for ye. Only—"

"Only what, Rachel?"

Her eyes fell again. "Only, ye know, John, I don't like this between you an' your father. It's wrong."

"Let that go," said John, and took her hand in his. "Let that go; 'twas to be. We'll manage, never fear. I'll work the hands off me to serve ye. We'll manage; maybe in a year or two I'd have more land an' better than what's gone."

"Oh, it's not that, John; it's not that. I don't mind the loss, or what's before us, or—It's not that. It's your being sent away, sent away wi' a curse on ye. It's this between you an' your father; it's because I'm the cause of it all. Oh, it's wrong, it's wrong!"

"Ah, whisht, Rachel; whisht! Woman dear, it's nothin'. Sure ye wouldn't have me give ye up? Eh? Would ye have me put father an' the land an' the rest all before you? Eh, Rachey?"

"No, no; but it's wrong, wrong. John, it mustn't be; it won't be; sooner than have such a thing on my soul, I'd go—I'd go an' never see ye again."

"Never see me again?" repeated John. He caught her face between his two hands, turned it to him and looked straight into her eyes. "What's all this, Rachel?" he asked.

"I mean it, John."

"Ye mean what?"

"I won't come between you an' your father, John; I won't have ye cursed an' turned out of home. Oh, can't ye see, can't ye see how foolish, an' miserable, an' wicked it all is? Can't ye see how sorry ye would be before long, an' how angry ye'd be wi' me, an' the struggle we'd have, the misery?"

John drew back his hands.

"Ah, that's it," he said, and, as lovers will (particularly your hot-headed kind), quickly changed from sweet to bitter; "that's it! You're afraid to face the world wi' me, afraid o' the struggle an' misery. This is what ye care for me!"

"John," said the girl, "don't be angry with me; try to see things as I do. God knows, my heart is sore; but—but there's no other way. Ye know—ye know how I care for ye, more than heaven an' earth. Ye know the sore, sore trial it is to me to have to say this."

"No, I don't," cried John; "I know no such thing. I've given up all for your sake; I come to ye for help an' comfort; an' ye turn from me."

"I don't, I don't. I want ye to do right an' to do right myself. Oh, surely, surely, John, there's some other way? Surely in time your father would see, an' forgive me, an' take the curse off ye?"

John jumped up, caught her hands, and pulled her to her feet.

"See here, Rachel," said he; "let's understand each other. You've heard what I've told ye. Ye know father; ye know me; ye know that whatever happens I'll not lower myself by goin' to him now for forgiveness. Are ye afraid? Or are ye goin' to give me up?"

"I won't do wrong, John."

"Answer! Will ye marry me, or will ye not?"

"John, I can't—I can't!"

John dropped her hands; turned and looked out across the hills—the hills which but a few hours before had shone so hopefully, and which now lay black beneath the hopeless night. Just to think of it! Over there, a lost inheritance; at his back, a faithless, heartless sweetheart; there, under the pitiless sky, himself, homeless and friendless! And this was the end? Good God! He turned and stretched out his arms. "I give ye one more chance," he cried. "Rachel Hoey, as I am, will ye marry me?"

There came back for answer only a broken sob; and mastered by black anger, John flung the reins to his tongue. This was the end of all. So much for women's word and vows!

Oh! but it had long been coming. She never cared for him. She had long wished to give him the go-by. Did he not see it? Who had sent her mother to anger his father and bring things to a climax? Ah, ah! Let her whisht!

"Ye needn't talk," cried John, this angry, foolish John. "I know ye sent her. Ye want me to go. Well, I'll oblige ye. From this night ye see my face no more. Ye hear that? An' you've done it, Rachel Hoey, mind ye. Of your own will ye've done it. Ah, the fool I was to trust your false, fickle face! May God forgive ye; may God forgive ye!"

And with that John turned, and closing his ears to the pitiful cry which came to him from the lover's seat beneath the old apple-tree: "Oh, John, John, come back, come back!" went out wrathfully into the night.

III

For long, in that night of misfortune, John wandered aimlessly through the silent fields; now cursing his fate, now muttering dark vows of vengeance, now, as the monstrous demon of his anger tore at his breast, shouting fiercely and shaking his clenched hands at the solemn stars; at last, near the time of dawn, found himself in the yard of his father's house.

For a moment his anger went. How came he there? he thought. He had no right now to a stone beneath his shoe in that yard; what devil of torture had led his feet thither? With an oath, he turned and slowly went down the lane towards the road; then, at the gate, remembering that at least he had a right to his own, wheeled suddenly back, boldly crossed the yard, and lifted the latch of the kitchen door.

Much to his surprise the door yielded. Very cautiously (for all his angry boldness) John stepped on tip-toe into the kitchen. Not a sound was there; not a sound as he opened the passage door and slipped up the stairs. Oh, home of John Hewitt's childhood, thus to have him enter you and, like a thief, go slinking for his own! You were born there, John; there your mother died; there your father sleeps, whose face you have vowed never more to see: through the long days of your youth and early manhood it sheltered you: now, like a thief, you glide through it, and only that little despised Mary up in her bare attic has ear or care for you! And it is all for the sake of a maiden—a maiden who has turned from you, my poor angry outcast!

Once in his room, John quickly changed his clothes, took his little store of money from a drawer, and noiselessly (for all his anger and bravery) started downstairs. On the landing he passed his father's door. It was open, and he peeped in. The dawn had come, pale and ghostly; there by the wall his father lay asleep. He could see the old white head; the texts on the wall; the open Bible on the dressing-table, with the spectacles lying across the leaves; the shelf above the bed, with its scanty stock of books and long rows of medicine bottles.

The demon plunged in John's breast. How could his father sleep there so calmly and his own son an outcast in the world, a friendless, angry outcast, obliged to sneak like a thief in search of his own? Oh, it was damnable! On tip-toe John entered. Black anger was on his soul. The demon was shouting Vengeance. There, there snug and asleep, lay the cause of all his trouble. Vengeance! Vengeance! cried the Demon; now! now is your time, a sudden blow, a sudden swift . . .

The first ray of sunlight shot across the dark counterpane, and turned to the colour of blood there before the young man's eyes. Blood! Murder! The word was blazoned all round the room. His hands flashed red before his face. With a cry as of a stricken animal, he turned swiftly, ran down, and out of the house.

And soon after, a little black figure also went out and followed in his footsteps.

Hardly knowing whither he went, and not much caring, John made across the fields, and before long struck the Bunn road. The sun was risen; its strong, fresh rays smote him with utter weariness; presently, he broke through a hedge, stretched himself in the shade of a haycock, and soon was fast asleep. And close by, that little figure in black watched and waited.

About mid-day John woke, sat awhile in deep thought (thinking, no doubt, though as yet with no very lively horror, of that horrible temptation which but a few hours before had come to him); at last rose, and once more took to the road. He was hungry and weary; the day was bright and gracious, but left him spiritless; in his breast anger was already nigh dispossession before the stress of a fine spirit of recklessness. An hour or two brought him to Bunn town, climbing white and straggling up from the tumbling river; and there quickly he sought meat and drink.

At that time a disastrous war was draining these islands of its manhood; and through most of our towns (through those, at all events, which, like Bunn, boasted a barracks among its public buildings) recruiting sergeants stalked proudly in scarlet and ribbons. That day, the quick eye of the Bunn sergeant, as he sat in the bar-parlour of the Diamond Hotel, winding his silver tongue into the dull ear of some hillside yokel, fell upon our outcast sitting forlorn over his meal in the corner. Here was his man, thought he; soon, having hooked his innocent, he was busy spreading the roll of glory before the listless eyes of John. Ah, the army was the place for your strong, clever fellow, your well-educated, handsome, big fellow; nowhere was promotion quicker or surer, particularly then in times of war; the life was noble, healthy; the girls ran wild after you.

"I say, sergeant," John broke in; "leave the girls alone, my son; ye'll not tempt me wi' them. Damn them! I say!"

The sergeant looked hard at John; then smiled knowingly to himself, called for more drink, and went on with his skilful tappings on the drum of Glory. Ah, the sport soldiers had, the free and easy life; no cares, no troubles, plenty of food and drink, plenty of devilment; and, at the end, a glorious return to friends and home.

"Never mind that either, sergeant," said John. "There's no home for me now, nor friends. I'm done wi' them, damn them one an' all! Divil cares I about wi' your shillin', my son, an' pass the liquor."

So John took the shilling; and at sight of it lying bright in his palm, an idea came to him, a brilliant idea, he was sure (as, indeed, it was bound to be, being born of anger and recklessness and the fumes of recruiting whisky); one which made him slap his leg, and laugh loud, and vow with an oath that the army was soon to receive a thundering comical dog.

"Easy a while, sergeant," said he; "take another glass till I write a scrape. Hi, there! More drink, an' that paper an' ink as fast as ye can. Now easy, my son, easy; I'll not be a tick, for the words are on the tip o' my tongue. Whisht now, an' don't spoil sport," said John, as, spreading his elbows and calling to his face a smile of supreme satisfaction, he began a letter; presently finished it, and with the shilling enclosed it in an envelope.

"Now, sergeant," said he, as with a great flourish he finished the address on the cover; "now, my son, I'm ready. Ye see that letter? Well, that's the finest joke I ever made, the very finest." (God forgive him, how often, afterwards, when lying weary and home-sick under foreign skies, did he think with wondering shame of that heartless joke.) "Boys, when that comes to the right place it'll make the man dance wi' rage. Och, och, but Irishmen are the play-boys, full o' fun they are. Look here, sergeant; this mornin' at daybreak—But no matter, that's all gone. I don't care a bucky now for all the fathers in Ireland! No more drink? Come on! Well, well, then; off we go—off for death or glory."

So the two swaggered out: and half-way down Main Street, just as John was turning into the post office, a little figure in black ran from a shop door and caught John by the arm.

"Aw, Sir, Sir," cried Mary, the servant; "ye haven't done it? Ye haven't 'listed? Och, don't say it! It'll brek me—me—Och, no!"

The sergeant laughed knowingly and turned away; he was used to scenes like that.

"Ay, Mary," answered John; "I'm off—off to the wars, my girl. The morrow or next day'll see me in scarlet red. But what brings you here, Mary?"

Mary's eyes fell.

"Ah," said she, "I—I—Master sent me a message. Ah, no, Sir," she went on hurriedly; "ah, no; don't leave us; don't, Sir. The master'll forgive ye. Come back, Sir. Ah do, for God's sake!"

John laughed down at the serious little face. "No, no," said he, "there's no forgiveness for me now, an' I want none. Good-bye, Mary, an'—Look here, take this letter to Father. Just give it him an' say nothin'. Good-bye, Mary; safe home, an' God be with ye!"

"Ah, no, no. Sir! Ah, no, no! I can't bear it. Ah, God ha' mercy! He's gone, he's gone, an' niver, niver will I see his face again! Ah; Mister John, Mister John, come back to me, come back!"

But John went on gloriously up Barrack Hill.

Some time that same day, a tax-cart, driven by an old man, as it turned off into the Bunn road, was met by a young girl. Quickly she stepped from the side-path and snatched at the reins. "Mr Hewitt," said she, "is John at home?" The old man looked down into the girl's pitiful face, all pale and worn with weeping. So this was John's sweetheart; this was the lass who had made him curse John, and disown him, and turn him from home. A bonnie lass she was, a bonnie—But John, where was John? "No, my lass," answered he, "he's not at home. But you—surely you—?"

"No, no," cried Rachel; "he left me last night, left me in anger. He said he'd never—Oh, Sir, where is he?"

The old man took his eyes from Rachel's face and looked slowly across the sun-lit fields.

Was he too late? he asked himself. Was his repentance too late? Was God now punishing him for his hardness and anger? Was John gone? Ah, that dream which had come to him at dawn that morning! His mind was full of it. For the hundredth time that morning, he saw again that pleading figure stand by his bed-foot, stretch out its hands imploringly, then turn from him, and with a great cry hurry from the room. And he had lain there in his obstinacy, nor moved a finger at the bidding of a righteous God! And now—?

He looked again at Rachel.

"God knows, my lass," said he. "God knows where John is. But come; jump up, maybe we'd both find him."

So these two, John's father and his sweet-heart, drove on together towards Bunn; and half-way there, Mary the servant stopped them, and delivered John's letter.

Very deliberately—for there was something like dread on his heart—the old man put down the reins and tore open the envelope. A coin dropped out, jingled on the bottom of the cart, rolled out upon the road, and was picked up by Mary the servant. Slowly the old man read the letter; then, without a word, handed it to Rachel.

Dear Sir,—she read,—Before you kicked me out of your house you swore to cut me off with a shilling. As I am sure you would begrudge me even that, and as I have no wish to be beholden to you for anything, Therewith enclose twelve pence sterling, being the amount which you have decided to leave me under the terms of your new will. I may add that the money has just been handed to me by one James Brown, recruiting sergeant of one of Her Majesty's Regiments of Foot. No receipt is necessary.

Yours, John Hewitt.

P.S.—You will never see my face again,

"Never see his face again?" cried Rachel! "Never!"

"Niver see him again?" cried Mary the servant, and clutched her shilling hard. "Is that what Mister John says? Aw, dear Lord, dear Lord!"

The old man picked up the reins and turned for home.

"Never see him again?" said he, as if to himself. "Never see his face again?"

And they never did; for in the wars John's portion was not glory.

THE HERD

I

It was a blustering day in early March; a day of racing clouds and fickle gleams of sunshine, a merry day, a hopeful day, a day that came shouting to men a glad promise of spring. You could feel it in the air, that message of life and mystery. It was in the wind, the sunshine, the rush of the clouds; you could smell it, see it, open your arms and crush it to yourself; it cried up to you from the sopping fields, piped to you in the naked hedges; it was there—and there—and there, mysterious, intangible, certain as life itself, the first flush and quiver of things on the face of a waking world. But only a flush, a message: for old Winter still reigned in the land.

It was of spring that the Master was thinking that day, as slowly he went splashing along the Curleck road down from Emo towards Kilfad and the shore; of spring, and work, and the ordering of things. His thoughts ran slowly, soberly, prosaically. That quiver of things made no turmoil in his heart, no ferment in his blood; his feet went heavily through rut and paddle; no vain beauty of sky or mountain tempted him to rise his head and look out across the hedges; soberly he walked along, hands clasped behind him, beard sweeping his breast, mind busy with thoughts of work—grim, unending work, and of spring—clean life-giving spring, with its gifts of sunshine and leaves, and warmth and hope and long days of fierce unresting labour. The winter had been hard and weary, the rains long and persistent; for months and months had the fields lain dead and the hills stood barren: but now, thought the Master, now spring was coming. He knew it. Instinct, feeling, something in the air, in himself, told him. He knew it. A few days more of bluster and sunshine, and the fields would be dry, the roads firm, spades busy, work going steadily. Involuntarily, the Master raised his head, flung back his shoulders, quickened his steps and to the merry lilt of a tune went splashing on his way.

He went through the oak plantation, crossed the Currach bridge (against the tumbled parapet of which, you may remember, George Lunny once leant his stilts whilst he looked at the moon), splattered through the puddles that lay darkly between the willow hedges; came presently to a gateway and, turning his back on Thrasna river, took to the fields—his own fields, the fields of Kilfad, famous from Gorteen to Bunn town for their grass and their mushrooms.

Along the pasture he went, whence sprang rushes three feet high from land that sagged to the foot like a filled sponge; skirted the Round hill (beyond which are Curleck woods and the home of Bessie Bredin); picked his way through a trampled gap, up a winding path, and coming to the crest of a slope there paused, turned, stood weighing his coat-tails and slowly sweeping the land with a long steady gaze.

The fields were empty, lying there among the hedges in their dull garb of winter, heavy and soaked to the lip. Not a beast moved within eye-shot, not a bird in a quickset; only a hay-rack standing far up the hillside, and the cluck of fowls round Jordan's cottage, gave evidence that life ran anywhere on Kilfad. Everything lay fallow, dreary, dead, thought the Master and looked out towards Gorteen and the long gleam of the mountain; everything, everywhere—the fields, bills, hedges, the grass, the trees, the houses even—lay there in the sunshine, dead and waiting for spring. For spring? Ah, yes; for the blessed spring, thought the Master; then turning again went on through the rushes and came to the cottage of Jordan the herd.

A long, low house it was, built of stone and white-washed; having a doorway in its middle, a small window on either side, and a single chimney springing from the thatch. Nakedly it stood upon the field, a lean-to at this end, a pig-sty at that; behind, a long narrow byre, a little pile of turf, a low butt of hay; here a hedge, there a row of poplars; in front, a trampled street, noisome and sprinkled with starveling fowls: no garden plot, not a bush or a plant, not a rag behind the windows, not a step even at the threshold, nothing anywhere but the chimney reek and the chickens in the mud to show that anything but beasts of the field had here found a home. Nothing but these and a very human sound of squalling that came with the smoke out through the doorway.

Sniffing and frowning, the Master crossed the street; came to the doorway and raised his voice. "Anyone at home!" he shouted. No answer came; none but a sudden hush within and a clatter among the stools. The Master came nearer, peered between the doorposts, called again. "Are you there, Henry? Are you at home, Ellen?"

Still no answer; then, in a minute, the soft fall of bare feet on the clay floor, a quick parting of the smoke-curtain, and there on the threshold—bare-legged and bare-armed, hair in wisps, face pale and worn, in her arms a baby, beside her and clutching at her tattered cotton skirt a flock of children—stood the figure of a girl. Not a word she said, not a sound came from the children; as if by magic the group appeared from the smoke and stood there motionless by the threshold.

The Master looked at them, sideways under his brushy eyebrows; then grunted and nodded at the girl.

"Oh, it's you, Jinny?" said he.

"Yis, sir." The girl's voice was soft, very timorous.

"You're not at school then, to-day?"

"No, sir."

"And why not?"

"I—I—Please, sir, I had to mind the childer."

The Master grunted again; looked towards the fields, caught his thumbs in his waistcoat pockets, turned again to Jinny.

"I know," he said. "And where is your father?"

"Please, sir, gone across the land with the billhook."

"I know. And where's your mother, Jinny?" asked the Master, looking full at the girl, both voice and manner curt with meaning.

The girl's eyes fell. She shifted the baby from this arm to that; flushed; looked up. "Gone to town," she answered haltingly, as from the verge of tears. "She's—she's gone to town."

The Master nodded. A grim look came to his face; his eyes grew stern.

"To town," growled he; then, with a glance at the girl, "And you're left here by yourself, Jinny! Left to mind the children!"

She shrank back a step into the curtain of smoke, and the flock of solemn-eyed children with her; shrank back, softly and silently, into the blue depths of the smoke. And as she went the curtain closed, her face went out, and her voice came murmuring. "Ah, yes, sir," it came; "ah, yea. But—sure—sure . . ."

The Master buttoned his coat; bent his head and entered the cabin. Before him the children scattered back, like rabbits from a keeper, and went scuttling through the pots and pans, the baskets and stools, which cumbered the floor. Jinny turned and ran, laid the baby in a box that stood in a corner, snatched up a chair, wiped it with a corner of her skirt and placed it by the hearth. Peering here and there through the drifting smoke—at the litter of a dresser, the chaos of a table—his head almost touching the rafters, his bigness looming giant-like in the little room, his feet wandering uncertainly over the floor, the Master crossed the kitchen, turned on the hearth, and stood with his back to the pots and the fire, face towards Jinny and the chair.

"No—no," he said, with a wave of his hand. "I won't be sitting, Jinny. I want to —When did she go?" he asked.

"Is it mother, sir!"

"Yes."

" 'Twas—" Jinny hesitated; moved away a little; stood fidgeting with her skirt.

" 'Twas a good while ago—after breakfast time—'bout ten o'clock mebbe."

"Yes!" The Master pulled up the chair, sat down with his arms resting on its back and his cheek in his hand. "Don't be afraid, Jinny," he said, his voice softening. "Come. Be a woman. And how did she go?" he went on, as Jinny looked up.

"On Bredin's jinnet an' cart, sir."

"I see." The Master paused a moment. "And she went by herself, Jinny?"

"No . . . No, sir."

"Oh, how's that?" The Master's tone of surprise seemed forced. "Who was it went with her, Jinny?"

"Please, sir—" Jinny stopped. A minute of silence fell. Not a sound came from the scattered children, cowering somewhere back in nooks and corners; not a whimper from the baby in its box. "Please, sir—" She stopped again.

"Yes, Jinny . . . Well? . . . Tell me. Jinny . . . Was it anyone I know?"

"Yes—yes, sir." A pause " 'Twas —" Another pause; then suddenly: " 'Twas Black Ned from beyond the lough."

And at that Jinny put face in hands and fell to sobbing.

The Master sat gripping his beard and looking sternly towards the doorway. He had heard only what he had expected to hear; still . . . "The hussy," he muttered to himself. How could she? What kind was she? "Oh, that tinker," muttered the Master; then turned quickly to Jinny. "But what's this?" he said. "What's this I hear? Come over to me, Jinny. What are you crying about?" asked the Master, and took the child by an arm. "What is there to cry about? Your mother will be back, you know. Maybe she's nearly back now . . ."

"It's not that," sobbed Jinny. "Oh, it's not that."

"Then what, Jinny? Tell me."

"What brings him here," cried the child. "What does he want? He's—he's always here. Couldn't he leave us alone? Ah, I hate him—I hate him," cried Jinny through her sobs. "I hate the face of him—an' the sight of him—an' the voice of him, I dunno—I dunno what it is; but—Ah, he means no good. I know it, I know it," sobbed Jinny; nor could the Master sitting there in his wisdom give back to the child so much as a word. "The hussy," was all he could say; "oh, the tinker." And so silence fell.

Presently, from the corners came a sound of stifled sobbing, from the box a voice that waxed swiftly to clamour and fury; Jinny ceased sobbing and stood looking at her hands; the Master woke suddenly to a perception of things, pushed back his hat and rose.

"Heigho," he sighed; then stepped from the hearth. "What's all this I hear, boys?" he called cheerily towards the nooks and corners. "Come, come; that's a poor noise to be making. Jinny's not crying: are you, Jinny?" He took her by the arm, led her to the doorway, and turned her face to his. "Never mind," he said; "be brave, Jinny, Do the best you can. Your mother will be home soon; if I meet her I'll hurry her. She must go to town sometimes, you know ... Anyhow, don't fret; and come up to Emo one of these days for an old dress or something I heard the mistress talking about. Come now—cheer up—and away in like a girl and see to the baby. Run now."

"I will, sir—I will."

"That's a girl." And the Master went

Turning towards the lake, he went through the fields, over the Round hill, across a footstick, and striking the Curleck road made towards Emo. His feet dragged heavily, his eyes sought the road. "The jade," he muttered at times; and again, "The tinker"; and again, "God help them all!" Very busy were his thoughts: but not now did they turn to work, or cattle, or the coming of spring.

Right at foot of the hill, where the road curves away from the river, sights the willows and makes straight for the Currach bridge; just there the Master stopped, raised his head and stood listening—with hands clasped behind him, shoulders slack and head twisted from the river, stood listening to an irregular thud of chopping, broken and smothered by a sullen roar of coughing, that came to him across the hedge. A minute he stood in the roadway, motionless and hearkening; then, groaning aloud as if in pain, mounted the ditch, put hands round mouth and shouted into the wind.

"Henry—Henry." The sound of chopping ceased. "Henry—Henry." The sound of coughing came, clearer. With his head bent to the wind, the Master stood on the ditch steadily eyeing the figure that came towards him across the grass.

A middle-aged man he was, big of bones and body, but woefully meagre of flesh, his eyes burning bright, face brick-red, a tatter of whiskers on his cheeks and iron-gray stubble on his chin. He wore tattered cord trousers, a sleeved moleskin waistcoat and a brown felt hat; from knee to boot his legs were wound about with ropes twisted from hay, round his neck was a long woollen muffler; his hands were chapped and scratched, his lips blue and dry, through the open front of his cotton shirt you had sight of his naked cheat. Slowly, awkwardly, one foot listlessly dragging after the other, this long arm swinging by his side, the other curled around the haft of a billhook, he came along the hillside; stopped before the Master and raised his eyes.

"Good evenin'," he said, with a nod. "It's brave weather."

"It is, Henry," answered the Master. "What are you doing over there?"

"I was hedgin'," came back, slowly, gruffly; "clearin' the briars. The ditch was choked," said the man after a pause; and again, "I wanted somethin' for the fire." He let the billhook slide through his arm, fixed the blade between his feet, leant his chest upon the haft and stood looking at the grass.

"Briars make bad firing, Henry," said the Master, looking towards the little pile of bramble that lay by the ditch out in the field.

"The worst," came back. "But they're better than nothin'."

"No turf, Henry?"

"Next to none."

"No sticks?"

"Sorrow a stick."

The man's manner was listless, slow, weary. He spoke with an effort, wasting not a word. His gaze across the field was bovine in its steady contemplativeness. From time to time he shook from head to heel with a paroxysm of coughing.

"Can you do nothing for *that*, Henry?" asked the Master at last, with a jerk of his head and a look at the heaving chest

"I've tried iverything."

"Been to the doctor lately?"

"I have."

"He said I'd make a fine ould man with a new pair o' bellows in me."

"Ah!" The Master pursed his lips, shook his head; looked away. "Wouldn't it be wise, Henry, to get a button on that shirt and wear a coat?"

"I dunno. Mebbe it might."

Nothing seemed of interest to the man. He stood there leaning on his billhook, just answering and coughing, waiting seemingly for nothing in the world but word to go.

"I've been beyond at the house, Henry," said the Master again. "I wanted to see you."

"Ay."

"I—I suppose the cattle are thriving!"

"They're doin' well—all but that red heifer. She's only donny."

"I know. And—I must come to see her. Yes." Somehow the Master seemed ill at ease. He had the air of one who beats about the bush. Then Henry turned.

"Ye say ye didn't see her when ye were over?" he questioned, wonderingly. "You passed them by an' niver looked at them?"

The Master stood accused. Never before in his life had he passed through Kilfad and not taken stock of all that lived upon it.

"I did," he answered. "I—I forgot. But—" He paused; then plunged. "Do you think it's wise, Henry, to leave those children over there by themselves—there with Jinny? Something might happen them . . ."

Henry pondered, still leaning upon the bill haft. "There might," he said, with a jerk of his head. "An' there mightn't," he added slowly.

"The children were crying, Henry," the Master continued, probing cautiously and watchfully. "Jinny came when I called. I went in." He stopped. Henry nodded; coughed; kept silent. "There was no one there but Jinny," said the Master. Henry stood gazing impassively at the hillside. The Master was foiled. "I suppose Ellen was out looking for firing!" he tried casually and with a smack of the ironical.

Again Henry nodded; pondered; spoke. "Mebbe she was," said he.

"Or gone fishing?"

"Ay, indeed."

"Or gone in Bredin's cart to town."

"Mebbe so," came back—that and not another word.

The Master wheeled away with a laugh and stood looking out across the big meadow towards Bilboa. He felt beaten, thwarted, puzzled. As well might he have talked to the ditch, or shouted at the Crockan there beyond the river. He had tried hints, insinuations; had been gentle, sympathetic, rough in the end and plain as a pikestaff: and all without avail. Nothing could touch the man. He was like wood. Something—trouble, or pain, or mortal sickness—had laid callous grip upon him, had blighted and left him joyless as a stricken tree. Had he feelings? Did he think? Did he know? Did he care for his children; had he fear for himself; did it matter to him a straw that Ellen his wife had gone elsewhere than for firing? Did he know; or was he ignorant; or had sickness numbed him; or was he only hiding behind this mask of indifference? The Master was puzzled. What was he to do, or say, or think? asked he of himself; and in answer found a great pity swell in his heart, rise and go out rushing towards that battered figure of a man. Pity? Oh, surely a dog must have given him that!

"Henry, Henry," cried the Master, "go home to your bed. Man, you're not fit to be out. Go home and let Jinny give you something to eat, and get to your bed . . . I'll send you something. I'll send for the doctor."

Henry turned his eyes, slowly, almost contemptuously.

"I want no doctor," he said. "There's nothin' ailin' me, nothin' but a bit of a cowld."

"Well go home, then, to the fire," pleaded the Master. "Do, Henry, like a man."

"I'm goin'," said Henry, and straightened his back, and pulled his hook from the clay, and stepped for his ditch; "I'm goin' when I'm finished. Yes."

II

The Master left the ditch and took again to the road. Soberly he trudged along, nor lifted his eyes from the stones at his feet. The day kept good; wind sporting, clouds speeding gaily, the sun flashing as he fell for the mountain; but in the day or its beauty the Master had no pleasure, had not even an eye, right or left across the willows, for the wide-spreading fields. Not often before in broad day had he walked blindly from Kilfad gate to the Currach bridge; never before, maybe, walked in greater turmoil of heart. He felt anxious, distressed; the hand of gloom was between him and the sun; he had a sense of foreboding; always before him, there between the ruts at his feet, stood that weary figure of a man, that unfortunate of a Henry . . . The poor life-crushed creature! Surely life was for him a pitiless road; death the sweetest mercy he might implore. Death—death—death! Was it comings-coming quick with the gathering months! . . . The unfortunate of a man! Something must be done for him; something those helpless children, that weary drudge of a Jinny; Something—but what? Something—but how? Help might be given them, bread, clothing, fire; but who might save them from themselves, their fate, their shame! . . . "Oh, the hussy," cried the Master within himself; "the jade." Why had he not long ago hunted her from the land, driven her out to seek her hind. She was a disgrace. The countryside reeked of the scandal of her doings. Her name was a by-word in the land, herself a pollution. And in his land! His! Oh, but this must end it, cried the Master, this day must end it all; then, in a flare of indignation, rounded a bend of the road, faced Emo hill. . . . and there before him was the woman herself. And with her the man, her companion.

In a narrow red and blue cart, drawn by a jennet, they came slowly down; the man driving, the woman seated by him on a plank that stretched across from edge to edge of the sideboards. The woman wore a brown shawl, black dress, large straw bonnet with long strings and a single blue flower; her face was big, heavy, flushed, with a low forehead and thick loose lips. The man was dressed in tweed trousers and waistcoat, a blue coat, brown hat and faded black and white necktie; he had a bad face, square, lowering, with narrow eyes that gleamed viciously. Both sat crouched over their knees, heads and hands forward, their bodies swaying in and out as the cart jolted. They looked sullen, dissipated. Not a word passed between them. At sight of the

Master coming uphill they sat upright; the woman with hands spread on her knees and lips a-quiver, the man plucking viciously at the reins and prodding the jennet with a stick. "Gwan!" he shouted, with a prod; "gwan to blazes out o' that."

The Master's first impulse counselled his standing aside to let them pass; his second born at closer sight of their faces, drove him to the middle of the road and left him standing there, legs spraddled, jaws set, thumbs hooked in the armholes of his waistcoat.

"Gwan," shouted the man, with a slash and an oath; "gwan to blazes out o' that"; then, to the Master, "Is it run over ye want to be? Stan' aside, then, or be the holy I'll level ye."

The Master stood firm; raised a hand. "Stop," he called. The cart came on. "Stop," shouted the Master; "stop, I say."

The man glared at him; then rose to his feet, storming and cursing.

"Stop," he roared; "ye tell me to stop! Ye dare order me . . ." The woman pulled at his coat-tails, crying him to be quiet. He turned upon her, his arm crooked as if to strike, his jaw set brutally. "You—you—" he shouted; then, turning suddenly, and with a storm of oaths, drew himself up and with all his strength smote the jennet twice across its back. The animal started, jumped; plunged forward. Just in time the Master sprang aside. "*Whirroo—whirroo*," roared the man, with a skirl and a twirl; the woman cried, pleaded, caught at his arms; the cart swerved, went clattering down the hill, swaying this side, jolting that, missing destruction at times by inches: so whirled round the corner, into the plantation, and was gone.

A while the Master stood on the wayside, rigid and quiet, with eyes looking steadily downhill; then, a sudden passion of anger rising within him, stepped out upon the road and went striding after the cart

"That's it," he said; "that's it! Oh, I'll show them. They dare—they dare—Oh, I'll teach them ... Out she goes—out she goes if I have to clear the house. The hussy. The jade ... If I can only come upon them; if I can only find that scoundrel in the house," cried the Master, and strode blindly between the willows. He was very wroth. His face was aflame, his hands hung clenched. To be scorned, insulted on his own roadway; spurned by carrion like that! Oh, he'd teach them a lesson for evermore ...

He saw the cart turn in from the road and go clanking slowly across the rushy field, the woman still seated upon it, the man walking by the donkey's head; saw it come to the trampled gap, saw the man flounder and fall, rise and fall: and seeing that the Master's anger cooled suddenly, and he stopped, bent his head and stood considering. This was a foolish business, he told himself; he was only wasting good breath and anger in chasing the wind. The man was drunk; the woman was drunk; she had tried to restrain the fellow; clearly, thought the Master, he had done wisely had he stepped aside and let them pass. Their business was none of his; they were hopeless and shameless: let them go, let them go ... But what of Henry? Of the children! Of little Jinny at home? Think of that child there in the smoke, shivering and hungering, waiting for she knew not what. Think of her feelings when she saw her mother stumble back, him who was with her, saw then sit there all the evening, drinking and singing, fighting and ... Oh, shame, shame, thought the Master; then passed the gateway, and went up the fields, and came to Henry the herd toiling patiently with his billhook on top of the hill. Not a moment did the Master waste.

"Look here, Henry," said he, catching him by the shoulder; "I told you to go home. Why haven't you gone! Come! No more nonsense; but go. Take up your bundle, I say, and go. You hear me!" said the Master, sternly and sharply.

Henry turned slowly. His eyes held a gleam of wonderment. "I do," he answered. "I do."

"Well go, then. And look here." The Master's voice took a less peremptory tone. "When you get home do your duty. You hear me? and do your duty. You hear me!" and swayed Henry to and fro.

"I do," came back; "I do, sir."

"Then off with you. There, take your bundle of sticks. And now your billhook—maybe you'll want it at home. Come, come," said the Master as Henry turned again on the hillside and stood gravely eyeing him beneath his hat brim; "I want to see you moving."

"But sure."

"I want no more words. I want you to be a man. I want you to go home. Come," ordered the Master; "take your billhook and go."

And without a word Henry turned, gave his bundle a hoist, tucked his billhook under his arm; and went trudging downhill towards home.

III

That night went, and the next day, another came and brought no sign; it was in the evening of that third day, the pitiless scourge of the rain having at last gone flying at burst of the sun, that the Master—now fallen somewhat anxious and curious not a little—turned once more from Emo gates and went down the Clackan road towards Kilfad. The road was deep. The hedges stood drenched and whipped upon the ditches, a diamond drop glistening on every thorn, leaked and gaunt rose the trees from rain-blanched fields—fields all sodden and dank, the grass upon them blue and beaten, the rushes drooping wearily. The hills shone, the valleys smoked in the sunshine, the lake glistened; over there, not a mile away you might think, stood the mountain, its face bright with a promise of coming rain. Rain! It was always raining, thought the Master. Spring? It was never coming—never. Look at the fields, the road, the floods; see the horizon bursting with rain; look at the world lying there in the sun, drowned in the eternal deluge. Ah, it was weary and hopeless, thought the Master, heartbreaking and hopeless; so, that mood of gloom lying black upon him, went through the plantation, and between the willows, and across the rushy bottom, and down along the path that led to Jordan's cottage. And as he went, down beneath the burden of his gloom, crept the haunting thought: *What did Henry do?*

Nothing moved about the house; nothing but the smoke above the chimney and the fowls upon the street the door was open; by the threshold stood a pot and skillet; beneath the kitchen window Henry's billhook lay rusting on the chopping block. The billhook! Hurriedly, and with something like dread on his heart the Master scattered the chickens and strode for the door.

"Hullo. Anyone at home?" No answer. "Henry, Henry. Are you there, Henry?" Still no answer, the Master stepped to the doorway, stooped, peered through the smoke; saw, in a minute, Henry by the hearth and the children round him, and he feeding them from a pot with their supper of porridge and milk. And seeing him the Master was glad; and he understood, and drew back, and waited patiently by the doorway, listening to the clink of spoon and bowl and idly watching the sky. Nor did the world seem altogether blank as he stood there, nor the spring altogether hopeless. For Henry's deeds, said he within himself, had not been desperate.

Presently the stools clattered back within, the children found their voices; across the floor Henry came clumping and issued from the smoke. He was bare-headed. His shirt sleeves were rolled to the elbows. His neck and chest were bare. His trousers were strapped about his knees, his naked feet showed within his unlaced boots. There was an ugly cut upon his forehead; one eye was blacked; his face, neck, chest were scratched and bruised. He looked flushed and hot; a little ashamed of his appearance.

"Well, Henry."

"Good evening sir."

"It's bad weather."

"The very worst."

"All well?"

"Ah, yes—iverything, thank God."

All this was pure trifling, beating for the hare. The Master turned.

"How are you, Henry?"

"Aw, the best." Henry coughed. "Sure I can't complain."

"Well you don't look the best." The Master eyed Henry's face and neck. "Has anything happened?"

"Ah, no." Henry paused. "Ah, no," he said again; "sorrow a thing."

The Master stood looking towards Emo. Henry leant a shoulder against the doorpost and stood rubbing his chin. Neither spoke for a minute; then, said the Master: "Is Ellen inside?"

"She's not."

"Where is she?"

"She's gone—gone to see someone."

Henry was lying; and the Master knew it. Why was he lying?

"H'm. I know." The Master paused. "What did you do the other day, Henry, when I sent you home?"

"Do?" Henry stared. "Do," said he. "What would ye have me do?"

The Master looked narrowly at him; laughed; then stepped and brought the rusty billhook from the chopping block.

"Look, here," said he; "I sent you home with this and I told you to do your duty. Did you do it?" Still Henry stared. "Did you?" repeated the Master.

"What's that?" came back. "Do what?"

"Did you use this"—the Master raised the billhook—"on the man you found in there?" He nodded towards the doorway; waited a minute for Henry's answer; turned and stood the billhook by the wall. "You weren't man enough to do it, Henry, I'm thinking," he said; "no, you weren't man enough."

Henry stood deep in thought, stolid, inscrutable as ever; then raised his eyes.

"Naw," he said; "naw, I wasn't."

"And why weren't you, may I ask!"

"Why?" Again Henry pondered. "Is it bloody murder you'd have me doin'?"

The Master could but laugh. It seemed all so absurd. Was the man knave or fool! He wheeled round and faced him.

"Look here, Henry," said he; "I don't understand you. If you're not playing with me you're doing something worse. Answer me this: Wasn't there a man in there on Monday when you came home? Wasn't there?"

"There was."

"And wasn't Ellen there!"

"She was."

"And they had whisky—and were nearly drunk—and just come from town!"

"Ay . . . Yes . . . Mebbe so."

"Well?" No answer. "Well, I say?" Still no answer. The Master stamped his foot. "Come!" said he, "enough of this. You must speak. I want to know what happened, and what you did. Come, sir."

The words were masterful, not to be denied. Slowly Henry moved his shoulder from the doorpost; stepped upon the street; stood looking across the fields. The wind flapped his flimsy shirt, stirred his hair. In the clearer light his face and neck showed thick with bruises.

"What is it I'm to say?" he asked, speaking slowly and plaintively and without turning his head.

"Just the truth. Just what you saw—what happened."

"I know." Henry turned, walked along the street; stopped at the end of the house with his face towards Emo. "It's the childer," he explained. "They seen enough; an' there's no use in them hearin' me." He stood blinking in the sunshine for a minute; then, abruptly and reluctantly, as one plunges when the water nips, began:

"When I got this far the jennet an' cart was standin' there on the street. There was nobody with it an' no one about. I put down me billhook there on the block, takes me bundle an' goes in. Well, things were stirrin'. The childer were bleatrin'—Jinny was cryin'—Black Ned was sittin' be the fire smokin' an' shoutin' at the childer—herself had her bonnet on her an' was getting tay. I takes no notice; but crosses an' throws me bundle in the corner; pulls over a stool and sits down. 'Twas all I could do. What could I do? Sure I was helpless. All I could manage was lift the child from the box an' try to quiet it. An' sure th' others got quiet too when they seen me, an' Jinny came over an' took a stool beside me. So thing weren't so bad—och, no. Only Ned was bleatherin'. He talked all kinds o' nonsense. He fair raved at times . . ."

"About me, Henry?" asked the Master.

"Aw, it was. 'Twas foolishness. Sure he'd been at the drink. No matter, anyway." Henry pondered a while; moistened his lips; plunged again. "Herself didn't say much," he said, speaking very deliberately and as one might speak with his face to the stars; "she was—she was busy gettin' tay. Ay. It was a big spread. I accuse Ned must ha' bought it all, else—Ah, I accuse he must. There was bacon an' eggs on the pan; there was lashings o' tay; there was butter, an' white bread, an' a pot o' jam on the table—aw, there was plenty of iverything, an' all of the best . . ."

"No whisky, Henry?"

"Ah, to be sure—a whole bottle o' John Jemison—a whole bottle. Ah, faith, I envied them that so I did." Henry shook his head, smacked his lips; a wistful look gleamed in his eyes. He sighed; continued. "Well, all bein' ready they drew up an' fell to on the bacon an' eggs, an' the tay, an' the white bread . . ."

"And the whisky, Henry?"

"Ah, to be sure. Is it leave that! . . . They set to, I'm tellin' ye, like a pair o' troopers; an' them laughin' all the time, an' singin' an odd tune, an' turnin' now an' then to fling a word at meself . . ."

"And you endured that, Henry?"

"Ah, to be sure." Slowly Henry made answer, as though he were speaking to the hedge, speaking of what hardly concerned him. "To be sure. What could I do? 'Twas drink—'twas drink. An' weren't there the childer, anyway, to be considered."

"Yes—yes. And they gave you none of the feast, Henry?"

"Not a morsel."

"Nor the children!"

"Not a taste—aw, not a taste. An' sure I thought that hard, for the wee cratures needed it. Ay, they did . . . Well, as I was tellin' ye, they ate an' drank an' sampled the whisky, an' had their diversion; an' after a while up Ned gets, an' makes for the fire, an' falls; an' herself tries to help him up, an' falls; an' they begin to squabble, an' the childer begins the cryin', an' Jinny catches howld o' me; an' there's a powerful whillaloo—chairs an' stools flyin', cans an' pots tumblin', the whole place in a ruction. Aw, 'twas a bad scene, so it was; 'twas powerful bad. I niver seen a worse—niver in me born days . . ."

"They fought, Henry!"

"Ay, like divils . . . 'Twas the drink."

"And you could do nothing!"

"What could I do! What could I do but save the childer from murder . . . 'Twas the drink."

"And then they made friends, Henry?"

"Ay. They did. They made it up an' got quiet again; an' after a while they went asleep, Ned lyin' on the table, an' herself wi' her head on a chair. I was glad o' that—sure I was—for the childer were hungry, the cratures, an' tired, an' dead wi' the sleep. So Jinny an' herself gives them a bite, an' takes them up to the room, an' puts them to bed, an' stops wi' them till they're asleep . . . I was glad o' that—yes, I was."

Henry stopped; drew his hand across his mouth; blinked slowly and gazed towards the Clackan hills. He looked starved and haggard in the broad light of evening. He turned to speak; hesitated; looked away. Patiently the Master waited, standing there with a smile playing on his lips and an incredulous look in his eyes. But Henry kept silent. Then said the Master:

"Well, Henry!" And again. "Well, Henry!"

"Aw, that's all—that's about all."

"No, Henry; there's more yet. Come. Tell me."

"Ah, it's nothin' . . . 'Twas me own fault . . . 'Twas the drink." Henry seemed questing for excuses. "Ay, 'twas the drink," he repeated, almost with satisfaction; " 'twas the drink." Again he paused.

"Go on, Henry. Finish."

"Ay, I'm goin' . . . Well, we got the childer to bed an' went back to the kitchen."

"Jinny and you!"

"Ay, the two of us. She wouldn't leave me. We went back, I'm tellin' ye, an' sat down again be the fire. We had a bit to ate. Then I lit me pipe; an' Jinny got out her needle an' set herelf to mendin' the childer's duds . . . an' there we sat an' sat just waitin' for somethin' to happen . . ."

Just waiting for something to happen. The phrase was so quaint, so pathetic nearly, that the Master had to turn away and laugh. It was a choice between laughing and crying. But Henry only paused a minute; coughed and went on, hurrying now as if to have done.

" 'Twas like this," he said. "After an hour or two I got a bit sleepy an' began noddin' on me stool; an' Jinny dozed a bit too; an' like that we were sittin' when all of a sudden Black Ned twists on the table in his sleep an' comes down slap on the flure. 'Twas like the end of the world the noise he made. I jumped that high—an' Jinny too—but it niver wakened herself, aw not a wake. Well, sir, Ned lay there for a while without movin'; an' just as we were wonderin' if he was killed, over he turns, scrambles to his knees, rises, rubs his eyes, looks round him, pulls out his pipe, lights it, an' without word or sign makes for the dure an' home . . . An' the heart rose in me at that—it did. For sure Ned's a terror in the drink—an' somehow I niver cared for him. Naw, I didn't . . ."

Somehow I never cared for him. The Master turned and looked Henry hard in the eyes. Was the man knave or fool? Was he crazed, as some said, by sickness and trouble? Did he know? Or was he feigning ignorance?

"Go on," said the Master.

"Well, after that," continued Henry, "we barred the dure, an' raked the fire, an' Jinny went to bed ... an' I goes over an' lifts herself's head off the chair an' shakes her awake, an' tells her to rise an' come to her bed. An' she rises an' looks at me, an' looks about her, an' goes up to the room, an' comes back, an' says she: 'Where's Ned?', 'He's gone home,' says I. 'Home,' says she; 'gone home? An' what took him home?' 'He went himself,' answers I; 'he fell off the table, an' got up, an' went home of his own free will.' 'It's a lie,' shouts she, 'it's a lie'; and wi' that flies into the ojusest tantrum you iver seen. Ah, 'twas terrible bad. Niver before did I see her in the like. You could hear her a mile. An' there was the childer all awake an' roarin', an' Jinny shiverin' be the dresser—an' herself ravin', an' cursin', an' accusin' me o' sendin' Black Ned home ... Ah, sir, but drink's the curse. She went fair mad ... An' at last she fell on meself, she came at me like a tiger an' bit me, an' tore too, an'—an' ..." Henry paused; shook his head. " 'Twas a sore case," he said; " 'twas a sore case."

What could the Master think! Seldom had he been in such perplexity. He could not fathom this puzzle of a man, could not decide whether he were deep or shallow, knave or fool. Did he know? Was he shielding her, hiding her sins beneath her faults, cloaking her enormities with his own weakness? Did he know? Was he telling truth? Was he guarding his tongue? Was he saying all he knew, or only all he chose to know, or merely all he was able to know?

"Well," said the Master. "Well, and what then, Henry!"

"Aw, she got tired at last," came back; "got tired at last—an' then she up, an' puts on her bonnet, an' goes out, an' slams the dure, an' leaves us there."

"Yes." The Master was watching Henry between half closed eyelids. "Well," he said again.

"That's—that's all."

"All! All!" The Master shouted the words. "But where did she go to!"

"I dunno." Very deliberately Henry answered, his eyes steady on the distant hills.

"You don't know! And you haven't heard from her! Haven't tried to find her?"

"Naw. Sure she'll come back herself; she'll be sorry an' come back."

What could the Master think, or say, or do! He laid a hand on the man's arm.

"Henry," he said; "answer me truthfully. Do you know where she's gone to?"

Henry considered. "Naw," he answered, "I wouldn't be sure, Mebbe it's to the brother's she's gone; mebbe it's to the cousin's beyond in Gorteen. But what matter, anyhow. Sure she'll come back—she'll come back."

"What could the Master think? Was the man speaking truth? Was he saying all he knew, or only all he chose to know? Was he lying to save her, to save the children, to . . .? Ah, what matter, what matter! Nothing mattered in sight of the look of truth and innocence that lived on that haggard face.

"You think she will, Henry?" said the Master, his voice softening strangely. "You think so?"

"Think?" Henry's face flashed round. "To be sure I do. Arrah, why not? What'd keep her away?" His voice swelled harshly; he stood flushed—roused at last. "Sure 'twas only the drink an' a fit of temper. To be sure she'll come back, an' the childer here waitin' for her—an' the house waitin'—an' Jinny—an' . . ." His voice softened; hesitated; drawled out.

"Yourself, Henry?"

"Ay. Aw, ay. What's left o' meself."

Henry turned; walked out among the rushes. And stood looking across the lake. Over there in Gorteen dwelt his wife's cousin, there too her brother; across there in Lackan, above on the hillside, dwelt the man—poacher, gaol-bird, blackguard—whose nickname was Black Ned. But it was always towards Gorteen that Henry looked—always and unflinchingly. "Ay," he said, and shaded his eyes, and looked steadily across the lake towards Gorteen; "what's left o' myself. Aw, to be sure she'll come back to us—to be sure . . ."

The Master dared not speak. He turned away and set out for home. And as he went, somehow life seemed bright with hope, the spring near and certain: and always, as he walked, had he clear vision of that battered figure standing there among the rushes, shading his eyes and watching for her who was sure to come.

Biography

John William Bullock was born in 1865 in Inisherk, County Fermanagh. He was the son of Thomas Bullock, steward of the Earl of Erne's Crom estate. After failing the entrance exam for Trinity College, Dublin, John Bullock briefly, and unhappily, tried farming before moving to London in 1883 to become a civil service clerk in Somerset House.

Taking the pen name Shan Fadh from the William Carleton story 'Shan Fadh's Wedding' Bullock supplemented his civil service income through literary journalism (he was the London literary correspondent for the *Chicago Evening Post* for twenty years). His short stories were published widely in magazines such as *The Outlook* and *The British Monthly*, as well as George Russell's *The Irish Homestead*. He published prolifically, including 14 novels and three collections of short stories, but his writing was never successful enough for Bullock to leave the civil service. However Bullock was widely respected by his contemporaries and played an active part in London's literary society. He was a friend of J.M.Barrie, and played for the Society of Authors' cricket team. Bullock also wrote a number of plays and one, 'Snowdrop Jane', was performed by the Ulster Theatre in Belfast's Grand Opera House in February 1915.

Between 1917 and 1918 Bullock performed secretarial duties, at the request of Sir Horace Plunkett, to the Irish Home Rule Convention, which was established to discuss self-government for Ireland. The Convention was overtaken by events as the Irish political landscape changed in the wake of the 1916 Rising, though Bullock was awarded a MBE for his role with the Convention.

In 1933 Bullock was made a member of the Irish Academy of Letters, which he regarded as the greatest honour of his life. He died in 1935.

Turnpike Books has been established to publish new editions of classic Irish novels and short stories.

Also available

THE LOUGHSIDERS

Shan Bullock

"One of the best novels that rural Ireland has provoked."
Benedict Kiely, *Irish Times*

Few writers have captured the comedy of country life, or the frustrations and daily struggles of small farmers, as faithfully as Shan Bullock. In *The Loughsiders*, Bullock drew on the speech, as much as the landscape, of the area around Lough Erne in his most complete novel with its understanding of the Ulster character and ironic observation of Ulster life.

Richard Jebb has returned from the United States to the quiet beauty, unchanging rhythms of life and close horizons of a small farming community along the shore of Lough Erne. Richard silently harbours larger ambitions and after his proposal to Rachel Nixon, the daughter of a neighbouring farmer, is refused he seizes his opportunity when her father dies without leaving a will. Complex and scheming, Richard manipulates the destinies of the Nixon family and his patient intrigue changes the lives of all those who live by the lough.